"Why did you say your name is Keira?"

Nick glowered at her. "None of your business."

"But it's not Delilah, is it?"

"No."

"You were out to seduce *me*, weren't you?" he accused.

"Now that is ridiculous!" Keira seethed with bitterness. "I'd never dream of being so hard-hearted, calculating, mean and despicable. Not like some people I could mention."

"I bet you thought you were seducing me—" his laugh was derisive "—and that's why you're in such a huff."

Keira looked Nick straight in the eye. "I think you're stupid."

"You're impossible!"

"Yes," she agreed calmly. "To you I always will be."

Something like an animal growl issued from his throat. "We'll see about that," he muttered fiercely.

EMMA DARCY nearly became an actress until her fiancé declared he preferred to attend the theater *with* her. She became a wife and mother. Later, she took up oil painting—unsuccessfully, she remarks. Then she tried architecture, designing the family home in New South Wales. Next came romance writing—"the hardest and most challenging of all the activities," she confesses.

Books by Emma Darcy

HARLEQUIN PRESENTS
1335—TOO STRONG TO DENY
1351—ONE-WOMAN CRUSADE
1385—THE COLOUR OF DESIRE
1401—RIDE THE STORM
1433—BREAKING POINT
1447—HIGH RISK
1455—TO TAME A WILD HEART
1463—THE WEDDING

HARLEQUIN ROMANCE
2900—BLIND DATE
2941—WHIRLPOOL OF PASSION
3085—PATTERN OF DECEIT

Don't miss any of our special offers. Write to us at the following address for information on our newest releases.

Harlequin Reader Service
P.O. Box 1397, Buffalo, NY 14240
Canadian address: P.O. Box 603,
Fort Erie, Ont. L2A 5X3

EMMA DARCY

the seduction of keira

Harlequin Books

TORONTO • NEW YORK • LONDON
AMSTERDAM • PARIS • SYDNEY • HAMBURG
STOCKHOLM • ATHENS • TOKYO • MILAN
MADRID • WARSAW • BUDAPEST • AUCKLAND

Harlequin Presents first edition July 1992
ISBN 0-373-11472-9

THE SEDUCTION OF KEIRA

Printed in U.S.A.

CHAPTER ONE

KEIRA MARY BROOKS wriggled her bottom. It was not a sensual wriggle. It was not a provocative wriggle. It was a desperate wriggle. Anything to ease the back-breaking, mind-numbing ache of being crammed into an over-small, over-hard, economy-class seat on a twenty-two-hour international flight that the travel agent had promised would save her a fortune.

Keira had known it was a mistake right from the beginning. How can you save a fortune when you don't have a fortune in the first place? The travel agent's spiel was obviously based on faulty logic. On the other hand, Keira had not exactly been over-loaded with choices. The price was right for her limited finances. She did feel, however, that the travel agent should have explained that the price was for the very worst seat in the Boeing 747.

She was jammed, literally jammed, in the middle seat, in the middle row, in the middle of the aero-plane; crammed between one elderly gentleman, so big that he had to be a retired wrestler, and one very overweight lady who, Keira mused darkly, would have had no problem getting accepted for a job in a circus.

Keira eased herself onto her left hip, gained some relief from the pressure on the base of her spine, felt eyes watching her, lifted her own to meet them. She had to lift her gaze a fair way because the watching eyes belonged to the big elderly gentleman on her left and her head only came up to his shoulder.

He looked stiff and staid. A walrus moustache added interest to his fleshy face. From the few words Keira had heard him speak over the past twenty-two hours, he had a British accent. He continued to stare. From the glazed look in his eyes, Keira figured that the long journey had broken down the famous British reserve and he no longer gave a damn whether or not it was rude to stare. Or perhaps his bottom was hurting, too, Keira thought sympathetically.

In any event, she was used to being stared at so it didn't worry Keira. In countries where people were generally dark in colouring, her hair had been the main object of fascination. For some genetical reason, it incorporated every shade variation from almost pure white to a deep yellow-gold. Its long, silky fairness was woven into a single thick plait over her shoulder at the moment, but it still seemed to strike people as something worth looking at.

By rights, Keira's eyebrows and eyelashes should also have been fair, but they were a light ash-brown, which tended to add an intriguing smoky emphasis to her green eyes. The retired British wrestler stared at her eyes for a long time before his gaze slid down her neat straight nose and fastened on her mouth.

Keira had a rather wide full-lipped mouth. It balanced up her high cheekbones and her squarish jaw line so she didn't mind it being a bit on the wide side, although she sometimes thought her face was all teeth when she smiled. She had noticed people seemed to get distracted by her smile. She tried to remember not to smile too much, but most of the time she forgot.

As she did now. The poor man had to be suffering, probably much more than she was, so Keira smiled sympathetically at him. He was holding a cup of coffee in his hands. Out of the corner of her eye, she saw the hot liquid spill over the rim and trickle onto his fingers.

"Sir, your coffee," she warned kindly.

The coffee slopped more alarmingly. The big man grabbed at his lap, emitting a cry of pain. He stood up, heedlessly dropping the cup on the floor as he brushed wildly at himself. He trod over people in his hasty plunge to the aisle, then charged towards the nether regions of the aeroplane.

"Sorry," Keira whispered, but in his anguish he didn't hear her.

It was an unfortunate fact that these nasty little incidents seemed to follow her around like a black cat, blighting the general happiness of her life. Keira heaved a deep sigh. She genuinely regretted what had happened to the big man. On the other hand, his abrupt removal gave her room to think without being distracted by the anguish in her bottom.

Keira stretched all her limbs, relieving her cramped muscles before luxuriously spreading herself across both seats. Thought was imperative. There was barely thirty minutes to landing, and the "fortune" the travel agent had saved her only amounted to the coins necessary for one telephone call and the fare for a very short taxi ride. One block at most, which wouldn't get her very far, and would leave a lot of walking at the end of it.

The telephone call was reserved for Justin. He was her cousin, an accountant, and a very cautious, conservative man. By Keira's standards he was also very wealthy, and in this particular situation her only chance of being saved from immediate penury.

He also needed careful handling. He was happily married, no children as yet, and Keira hadn't seen him for five years. But she knew his habits. He liked to get sheets of paper, write down figures on them, add them up, then draw conclusions from them about which he lectured her interminably.

Keira's view was much more simple. Family always sticks together through thick and thin. Blood is thicker than water, and a lot thicker than nasty little numbers on a page. At which stage, Justin would run his fingers through his thinning hair and growl. The problem with Justin was that he wanted family and numbers to add up correctly all the time. And they just didn't. Not with Keira, anyway. Justin had a lot of difficulty coming to terms with that.

Like the time he sent her the money to return home for his wedding. Keira would have gone—family first above everything else—but she had been on safari through Kenya, which was where she had met the sheikh, who had kindly invited her to Morocco, and by the time the post with the invitation and the cheque caught up with her, the wedding was over. What was the point in flying to Australia when Justin and Louise were already on their way to Fiji for their honeymoon? They never would have met, so there was no point at all! Only Justin didn't seem to understand that.

Keira had posted the cheque back to him with profuse apologies, explanations and congratulations, but communications between them had definitely been strained by the incident. Although he hadn't written it straight out, Keira had been left with the forceful impression that Justin considered she had LET HIM DOWN. From then on he only sent dutiful birthday and Christmas greetings, with the somewhat sarcastic postscript, "Are you still alive?"

Keira had regularly assured him of her continued survival with postcards from every country she visited. Which brought her to the problem of how to approach the conversation when she made her all-important telephone call. The opening phase of communication could be decisive. After all, Justin thought she was still in Reykjavik, Iceland. *He would be surprised.* And Justin didn't react well to surprises. So perhaps . . .

The big man reappeared from the nether regions of the aeroplane. His face was fixed in an attitude of interminable suffering. With a rush of true compassion for him, Keira relinquished the extra space. This kind of travel, she thought, was the end.

Which went to show it *was* time to come home, or she wouldn't have thought that. A few years ago she would have happily camped on the deck of a tramp steamer to get somewhere new. Now she longed for a bit of home comfort. She hoped Justin would provide that for a little while until she got on her feet again.

The No Smoking sign flashed on. Fasten safety belts. Ten minutes to landing. Keira recollected that she hadn't decided how to handle Justin. She shrugged. Perhaps it was best to simply leave it in the lap of the gods. Play it all by ear.

From her disadvantaged position in the middle of the aircraft, she caught only glimpses of Sydney as the plane banked to make its approach into Mascot Airport. Even so, the distinctive features of her home city triggered a ground swell of feeling that caught Keira by surprise.

It's true, she thought. There's no place like home. Over the past five years she had travelled the world and left bits of her heart in many places, but when it came right down to the bone, she was a born and bred Australian and her native land claimed first and last place in her soul.

The plane landed and the long flight was finally over. Disembarking was an exercise in enforced patience, but Keira was soon able to stretch her legs on the walk through the tunnel into the terminal. Having collected her backpack and duffle bag from the baggage carousel, she had to suffer another long queue at customs.

At last she was free to find a telephone and call Justin. It was six-thirty in the morning. Thursday morning. He should be home. Keira dialled his number, then felt a nervous kick of anticipation as the click of a lifting receiver cut off the call pattern.

"Justin Brooks," came the gravelly grunt of displeasure at being wakened. The tone clearly implied that any decent upstanding working person deserved his full rest, and whoever was calling had better have a damned good reason for it.

Keira grimaced an apology, which unfortunately he couldn't see, and pitched her voice to a soft croon of appeasement. "Dear darling Justin, it's Keira, your beloved wayward cousin."

Incredulous silence.

She pitched her voice to what she hoped would be sympathetic appeal. 'I'm sorry if I woke you...."

"Time differential," he muttered. Then with a note of urgency, "Where are you? What part of the world?"

He actually sounded concerned about her. She hadn't expected that. "I'm home, Justin. At least, I'm here in Sydney. At Mascot Airport."

"Thank God! Don't move an inch! I'll be there straight away!"

Keira was dumbfounded. She had hoped for a response, prayed for a response, but this example of cousinly love was more than she had expected . . . or ever experienced before.

"Are you sure, Justin?" she asked uncertainly. "I mean, I can wait—"

"No!" Explosively positive. Or negative. Keira felt a bit confused until he added, "Don't you dare move! I'm coming straight away. I'm out of bed already. I'll be there in thirty minutes maximum. You are not to go haring off somewhere. Do you hear me, Keira? For once in your crazy wandering life, stay put!"

Things were really looking up. Perhaps Justin's idea of family loyalty had changed for the better. "Well, if you insist—"

"I do! Promise me you won't move!" he commanded.

Thirty minutes was a long time to stay absolutely motionless, and her mouth felt like a desert. "Am I allowed to have a cup of coffee at the cafeteria?" she asked cautiously, not wanting to put him off his stride.

"Good thinking! I'll find you there. Sit down and don't move. Oh, and Keira—" the bossy voice wavered into anxious uncertainty "—you haven't got fat, have you?"

Strange question! Her eyebrows shot up. "No. I don't think so. What's the matter, Justin? Have you got a skinny car now?"

"Checking. Just checking. It has been five years. Am I going to recognise you?"

"Same as I ever was," she answered breezily.

"Great!" A huge sigh of relief. "I need you, Keira. You can't let me down."

"Oh, I wouldn't do that, Justin," Keira assured him fervently. "I, uh, need you, too."

"Perfect!" A smug note there.

"Perfect for what?"

"I'll fill you in when I see you."

The receiver was decisively slammed down. End of conversation. Keira hung up her receiver in a state of bemusement. Justin had never needed her in his life before. In fact, he had always seemed to find her a disturbing or disruptive force. She was almost sure he had resented her intrusion into his family household when her aunt and uncle, his parents, had taken her in after her own parents were killed in an auto accident.

Keira had been ten then, Justin fourteen, and even in his teens he had liked everything orderly and predictable. He had always acted the responsible big brother, but the truth was, they had never shared a common wavelength, and Keira suspected Justin regarded her as a cross he had to bear for the sake of family. Now that she was twenty-six and he thirty, things might be a little different, but somehow Keira doubted it.

Whatever the reason, it was lucky Justin needed her, because she certainly needed him. It was indeed a perfect resolution to her temporary problem. She didn't understand why it was perfect for Justin but no doubt he would soon enlighten her. Meanwhile a cup of coffee would go down well.

As Keira headed for the cafeteria, she couldn't help wondering what fat had to do with anything. Justin certainly wasn't thinking straight. How on earth would she get fat trekking around the world on a slim budget? She was in great shape. Quite a few men privately agreed with her as she went striding through the terminal.

Their eyes were caught by the fascinating jiggle of her full breasts, which turned her man's cotton shirt into an incredibly provocative garment. Their heads swivelled as she passed by, drawn inexorably to appreciate the way her stretch denim jeans moulded the trim, taut, cheeky femininity of her bottom. Keira was still trying to work out the numb ache, and the rolling movement she used was positively mesmerising.

That, in turn, drew attention to her long, lissome legs that should have been sexily encased in high-heeled calf-length boots. Her sturdy army boots, so practical and comfortable for walking long distances, earned disapproving frowns.

Keira, however, was blithely unaware of these cursory appraisals. Her mind was filled with the blissful thought that she could afford a cup of coffee with a clear conscience. All was temporarily right with her world. Justin would certainly feed her and put a roof over her head if he needed her.

Having found the cafeteria and paid out the last of her hard cold finances on a steaming cappuccino, Keira settled at a table and considered the situation. First she would oblige Justin with whatever he needed her for. She hoped he would be suitably grateful enough to lend her the money to visit his parents, who had retired to the Gold Coast of Queensland. Then she would look around for a job.

She wondered what Justin's wife was like. He hadn't mentioned Louise on the telephone, but no doubt she was now warned her cousin-in-law, the prodigal one who had missed the wedding, was about to descend upon them and mess up the neat orderliness of their lives.

Maybe Louise was sick, and that was why Justin needed her in such a hurry. Or maybe his mother or father was sick and they needed a helping hand. Keira worried about that for a while. Auntie Joan's last letter had assured her that all was well at home, but it was not in Auntie's nature to worry anyone. Keira automatically discounted the idea that Justin needed her himself. That was totally beyond the realms of even her inventive imagination.

Suddenly she spotted him, hurrying towards the cafeteria. Her eyes widened in shocked surprise. Justin hadn't stopped to shave! Unbelievable! Appearing unshaven in public indicated a crisis of maximum proportions. Though he had managed to dress in conservative grey trousers and a conservative white shirt. On the other hand, he probably didn't own any other colours.

His forehead was a little higher on account of his light brown hair having receded a little farther. From her seated position, Keira couldn't see if it was any thinner on top. His face looked more or less the same. It was actually a good-looking face and Justin could even be called handsome when he smiled, but his smiles were very rare, and right now he wore a harried anxious expression. There was no flab on his tall well-proportioned physique. Had he developed a fastidious obsession against fatness? Keira wondered.

His face positively lit with relief when he saw her. It was almost as good as a welcome. Keira gave him her warmest smile. His brown eyes beamed approval at her. *Approval* from Justin? This meeting was getting curiouser and curiouser by the second.

"Am I glad to see you!" he enthused as he arrived at her table.

"Likewise!" Keira replied brightly. "Am I allowed to move now?"

He pounced on her backpack and duffle bag as though they were hostages for her continued good behaviour. "Yes," he said. "Best if we get going."

She stood up and planted a cousinly kiss on his raspy cheek. It really was nice to see him, even though their minds worked on different wavelengths. It made her feel even more at home.

"It's so kind of you to come and collect me like this, Justin," she said with sincere gratitude.

His face went grim. "These are desperate times in which we live."

"Precisely," she agreed with feeling.

He frowned at her. "Are you tired, Keira?"

"How far away is the car?"

"It's just across the road in the car park. No great distance. Maybe a hundred metres."

"Lead on," she invited. "I am suffering a broken backside but I can get myself that far."

He watched her walk beside him for several anxious moments, checking that her mobility was not too impaired.

"Are Auntie Joan and Uncle Bruce all right?" she asked, wanting that worry settled.

"Mum and Dad?" he said distractedly. "Same as usual. Fine as far as I know."

No problem there, Keira thought in happy relief. She was very fond of Justin's parents. They had never understood her, but they had never criticised her, either. Their attitude towards her was one of benevolent tolerance. Occasionally they likened her to her father who apparently had nursed a wanderlust when he was alive.

"Will you be right for tonight?" Justin suddenly asked.

"For what?"

A look of black thunder passed over his face. "A man," he said, and there was no benevolence at all in his tone of voice.

Keira had the forceful impression that the man in question did not bask in Justin's favour. "What kind of man?" she probed warily.

His mouth curved into a sly little smile. "No-one you'd object to, Keira. Most women seem to find him charming. You might even feel attracted to him. He's reported to be a very eligible bachelor."

Interesting, Keira thought. "What do I have to do?"

The smile turned into a smirk. "Oh, be yourself. As much as you can."

There was something fishy about that smirk. Justin was never comfortable with Keira being herself. Her attitude to life offended his sense of precision. "Is that all?" she asked suspiciously.

He cast her a stern look. "You definitely *must* forget that you're my cousin. That is essential."

Keira didn't care for that idea. After all, it was essential to her that Justin remember he was her cousin.

"Apart from that," he continued, "all you have to do is try your best to seduce him. I want him compromised. Past the point of no return."

She couldn't believe this! "My God, Justin! What do you think I am? You actually want me to seduce a man?"

Justin nodded with smug satisfaction. "That will certainly turn the tables." Then he had the thick hide to offer her a sympathetic look. "I'm sorry about your broken backside, Keira, but you have all day to rest and get some sleep. You should be fit by tonight."

She took a deep breath. Maybe all the rushing around so early in the morning had made Justin light-headed. "You really want me to seduce a man I've never met?" she asked, still not believing he could be serious.

"You've had enough practice," he said glibly. "Shouldn't be difficult for you."

Keira's jaw dropped. She gasped at him. A surge of indignation effected a fast recovery. "I have not! I've never done such a thing in my life!"

He slanted her a wise look that denied any belief in her protestation of innocence. "Well, see if you can get some practice tonight," he advised.

Keira shut her mouth. This was not the time for confrontation. She certainly wasn't going to seduce anyone, not for love nor money, but it wasn't at all practical to say no right now when she still needed Justin's help and support. Appeasement, Keira thought. She'd sort out what was going on eventually, then wriggle out of it somehow.

"I don't think I understand this, Justin," she said in a befuddled tone.

"It's quite simple." He threw her a knowing look. "Fight fire with fire. Elementary. I'm doing the fighting. You're the fire. Couldn't be more perfect, really."

Keira shook her head. "I'm sorry, Justin, but this sounds like you're stretching family obligations past a reasonable point."

"Not at all, Keira. This is family. All family," he argued with considerable vehemence. Almost passionate vehemence! "Do this one simple thing for me and I'll be obliged to you all my life. Longer. For eternity. That's family!"

His brown eyes stabbed encouragement at her. "Do you want me obliged to you all your life, Keira?"

It certainly had its attractions. As a backup for emergencies, to have an ever dependable support like Justin was not to be scoffed at. Even so, Keira wasn't about to sell her body for the sake of security.

"It would be nice," she answered cautiously. After all, they weren't quite out of the airport yet. They were only crossing the road to the car park. She didn't want Justin to dump her bags and leave her flat.

"Then do it!" he concluded decisively.

Keira temporised. "I think I need a few more details, Justin. I mean, if I'm to get this right for you...."

He sighed, putting on his lofty superior face. "Keira, there's no point in explaining the details. You can't follow a simple budget let alone a complex equation. This is much more difficult. Just do precisely what I say when I say it."

He gave her a hard, warning look. "You are you. I recognise that. But for the next few days you are not to let things happen to you, Keira. You are not to improvise, or ride along with some tide of opportunity. This is a perfectly planned military operation. I'm the field marshal. You're the private. I give the orders. You go out and die for honour, glory and happiness."

Dying was definitely out as far as Keira was concerned. No-one's honour, glory or happiness meant that much to her. "This all sounds pretty one-sided to me, Justin," she said pointedly.

"Do you want my eternal gratitude?"

He dumped her backpack and duffle bag on the pavement behind a Daimler. Justin had owned a Ford Falcon five years ago. Now he had a Daimler. His stocks had definitely gone up in the world. A lot of home comforts flashed across Keira's mind.

"Yes," she said.

"Then that's settled. You're the private. I'm the field marshal."

Keira allowed the field marshal to stow her baggage in the Daimler's boot, then see her settled into the beautifully comfortable passenger seat. Her bottom was very appreciative. Lovely luxury, she thought. Being a private was not entirely bad, but obeying orders—Justin's orders—was a highly questionable area.

She waited until he had the car on the road, then asked, "Are you sure the plan is going to work, Justin?"

"That's my worry. Not yours," he said with pompous authority.

"But you will be grateful for my help."

"I promise."

"Grateful enough to give me a loan?" This was very definitely the time to introduce the practicalities of life.

Justin winced. "How much?"

Keira did some quick figuring, then tripled the amount for good measure. Justin bared his teeth at her, then divided the figure by six and came up with five hundred dollars.

Keira winced. "Justin, that would hardly keep body and soul together for longer than, um, a few days."

"The rest on delivery," he said with a look of triumphant satisfaction.

Nailing her down to his orders, Keira thought in disgust. No trust at all. So much for *his* family feeling!

"What am I to deliver before I get the rest? This man's head on a plate?" she asked sarcastically.

"That would be eminently satisfactory," he said, without so much as cracking a smile. He looked as though he meant it.

"So I'm supposed to be a modern-day Delilah?"

"Exactly."

"Why?" she demanded to know.

There was a rush of blood to his head. His face went a dark red. He glared at her. "Because I want my wife back! And you're going to help me do precisely that."

Shock rippled through Keira's mind. It was followed by a burst of clarity. Louise had obviously run off with another man. Poor Justin *was* in a crisis. She certainly had a family obligation to help him.

"After all," he argued hotly, "if you can take off with an Arab sheikh and miss my wedding—"

That still rankled.

"—you can take off with an Australian playboy and save my marriage!" he finished triumphantly.

Keira smothered a sigh. Justin was upset. He wasn't thinking straight. For one thing, he really did have the wrong idea about her association with the sheikh, which had nothing whatsoever to do with seduction. And *his* campaign to get his wife back was sure to be disastrous. It was perfectly clear that she would have to sort it all out for him. Men simply didn't understand women. And they never really listened to them, either.

Subtlety, Keira thought. Justin didn't have any appreciation of subtlety. No point in arguing. She would have to show him. Maybe after *his* plan failed, he would begin to listen to her and really see, for the first time, what she could do.

CHAPTER TWO

KEIRA DID NOT let Justin down.

She did everything he told her to do.

She even accepted the alias Delilah O'Neil. Justin was adamant about that. He wouldn't accept anything else. In Keira's opinion, this was stretching cousinly love to its outermost limits. However, Justin argued that Louise knew he had a cousin called Keira, and Delilah O'Neil was a name he could remember. At all times. It was also rather unusual, he said, and would draw attention to her.

She accompanied him to a dreadfully overcrowded party, hung on his arm, looked adoringly at him as ordered, showed him how to loosen up with several new dance steps no-one else seemed to know—inadvertently stirring considerable interest amongst onlookers—and generally fulfilled the role of the blonde Biblical bombshell that Justin required of her.

He refused to point Louise out to her. Louise was to be ignored. Keira began to suspect Louise wasn't at the party at all, because Justin didn't point out *the man* to her, either. This gave Keira much secret relief because she really didn't know anything about seducing a man, not deliberately anyway, and she couldn't go along with that part of Justin's plan.

Then it happened.

The big moment.

The one she had given up believing would ever happen to her. She had travelled the world, met thousands of men, but never once had any one of them awakened any special recognition in her heart.

She didn't see him coming. There was a voice behind her, low, soft, seductive. "Please don't spoil the magic for me. Tell me you're intelligent as well as stunningly beautiful."

She looked around, drawn by the voice, unsure if the words were spoken to her or someone else. And there he was, blue eyes twinkling at her, blue eyes dancing through her brain, tripping her heart, sending a zing of excitement through her veins.

He was half a head taller than Keira, over six feet tall. His hair was midnight black, a stylishly tamed mass of waves and curls that gave a rakish air to his handsome face. A devilishly handsome face, darkly tanned and composed of sharp planes and angles that were distinctively masculine and intriguingly attractive. Black eyebrows were lifted in a wickedly challenging arch. His sensual mouth was pursed in teasing invitation, slowly widening to a dazzling white smile.

He held two glasses of champagne in his hands and he offered one to her. "I know your escort is at the bar. I know we haven't been introduced. I know I am intruding on what is forbidden ground. But there are no rings on your fingers and the thought came to me that someone should look after that. So I beg your indulgence. If necessary...your forgiveness...for this intrusion."

He was playing with words. There was no hint in his eyes of needing forgiveness. Self-assurance surrounded the man like the aurora borealis. Keira dazedly took the glass he offered her. Their fingers brushed. Something like an electric charge ran up her arm.

"Speak to me," he commanded. "I need to hear your voice."

Keira smiled. She couldn't help herself. "You've been saying the same thing to every attractive female you've met since..."

She dropped her gaze to measure a suitable height from the floor. He wore an open-necked shirt of fine white linen, pintucked and expensively tailored. Black moleskins hugged his lean hips and muscular legs. Somehow his body emitted a raw sexuality that was all male animal. The physical impact of the man was like nothing she had ever felt before. Keira almost forgot her train of thought. She belatedly fixed her gaze at mid-thigh, surveyed the area intently, then looked up at his vividly inviting blue eyes.

"Uh, I'd say, since you were five years old," she concluded.

He laughed, warming her with his pleasure and delight. "You know me so well already. I must offer you every opportunity to further your knowledge. Ask anything you want of me. Whatever is possible, or impossible, shall be granted."

"That's a rare offer. Perhaps a little rash? You don't know me. I might ask for the moon and the stars."

"Then you'd have them. From me. With compliments."

"How?"

"I'd take you away from this maddening mass of people to somewhere private, personal, quiet and peaceful, and open to the sky...a yacht, a beach house, a mountain chalet. You choose," he invited. "Whichever you want can be yours."

She laughed. The sheer fantastical extravagance of his offer appealed strongly to her own sense of spontaneity. "You can conjure such places up with your Aladdin's lamp, can you?"

"I don't have to. I own all three," he assured her with such arrogant confidence that Keira was inclined to believe him.

It gave her pause for thought. She lifted her glass and sipped the champagne while she reassessed him. Her heart and soul were engaged. They were pulsing with very positive messages. He was THE ONE. But there had been a lot of women in this man's life. Did he recognise her as the one for him? Was he seriously attracted to her, or was he simply throwing her a line, having decided to sample someone new?

"You must be a very wealthy man," she remarked.

"Very," he agreed nonchalantly, but there was a flash of hardness in the blue eyes.

"You think I can be bought?" she challenged, pitching her voice to light mockery.

One eyebrow lifted quizzically. "Can you?"

She lowered her long thick lashes as though for private thought and consideration. She secretly enjoyed making him wonder before she answered with a flat, "No."

He smiled...slowly, lazily, winningly. "Then I don't think it."

Keira's heart pitter-pattered all over the place. She took another sip of champagne to settle the palpitations. It failed to achieve that purpose because he lifted his free hand and trailed his fingers through the long tress of hair that had fallen forward over her left shoulder.

"Spun silk," he murmured. "I've never seen anything like it before."

Justin had not allowed Keira to rest the entire day. At four o'clock he had taken her to a hairdressing salon to have her hair shampooed and blow-dried and any ragged ends trimmed to the one shining length that flowed to below her shoulder-blades. He had insisted that she leave it loose, which was a nuisance for dancing, but suddenly Keira felt Justin had got something right. His judgement wasn't all bad. Not all the time.

On the other hand, she wasn't just a head of hair, and when its admirer lifted a swathe to his lips, Keira experienced such a frightening tide of sensual excitement that she voiced a protest. "You take a liberty, sir."

He breathed in its scent before allowing it to slide from his fingers. "Guilty as charged. I'll accept any punishment from you except banishment," he replied, his eyes wickedly daring her to make some outrageous claim on him.

"If I say you're not to touch me again?" she challenged, unable to resist testing him.

"Unacceptable. That is banishment."

"Do you always make the rules?" she asked.

"I spend most of my time breaking them."

"Not a conservative man."

"No more than you're a conservative woman."

"Why do you say that?"

His eyes simmered with a heat that curled right down to Keira's toes. "I watched you dance." He took the champagne glass from her hand, placed it on the mantel behind her, transferred his to the same place, then curled his fingers around hers in a possessive grip. "Come dance with me. I'll show you we're made for each other."

He didn't wait for her consent, but began leading her through the crowd.

She shouldn't, Keira thought. She shouldn't move from where Justin had left her while he got them drinks from the bar. She shouldn't be letting any of this happen at all. Justin had laid down the law. No riding a tide of opportunity.

But this was the big one, Keira argued to herself. The king tide! It wasn't her fault that Justin had messed up the love of his life. He couldn't really expect her to pass up what might be the love of *her* life. That was totally unreasonable. Not even Justin could be that unreasonable, could he?

She looked back, trying to spot him, wanting to catch his eye with an apologetic appeal, but she couldn't see him. Only one dance, she told herself, needing to appease an uncomfortable stab of guilt. She had promised not to let Justin down, and she wouldn't—but one dance couldn't hurt too much. And then... Well, she would have to wait and see.

Besides which, if Louise and her man weren't here, what harm could this little desertion of duty do? It was only one dance.

She allowed herself to be led out to the huge tiled patio that spread from the main entertainment room to the swimming pool. Keira didn't know whose house this was, or why the party was being held. Those items were not on Justin's need-to-know list. But it was a magnificent home and ideal for entertaining on a large scale. Justin's social circle had apparently zoomed up with his stocks.

Music was supplied by quadraphonic speakers set around the patio. A track from Michael Jackson's *Thriller* was being played. The strong hand holding Keira's pulled her closer as the man to whom it belonged turned to face her.

"Make your own rules," he invited, the blue eyes glittering warm anticipation. "I'll follow."

Every instinct warned Keira that this was dangerous. He was not a follower. He did not ride along with opportunity. Nor did he let it pass by. He seized it and made it his. Yet the sense of danger only served to heighten the excitement he stirred in Keira. She wanted to know how well he could dance, whether he could match her.

To give Justin his due, he had tried, but he didn't really feel the rhythm. He was too inhibited to let his body flow with it. Too uptight. Too conscious of his dignity. Too civilised. But Keira knew intuitively there would be no holds barred with this man.

She moved back to give herself space. He watched her, waiting, his body poised, ready to respond to any movement from hers.

Keira was wearing her little black dress, a designer original she had picked up very cheaply from a second-hand shop in Paris. It was made of some magical fabric that could be rolled up into nothing and stored in a pocket of her duffle bag. Keira had worn it innumerable times. It was ideal for any special occasion and perfect for dancing.

The style was very simple. The close-fitting bodice was cut on the bias, moulding the fullness of her breasts in such a way that a bra was unnecessary. Shoestring straps supported a low heart-shaped neckline. Around her trim waist she wore a gold chain. The plain circular skirt fell from just below her hips, giving her legs free mobility. High-heeled black sandals were strapped securely around her slim ankles.

He was waiting for her to start fast, Keira thought, as she let the rhythm beat into her mind and through her blood. She decided to completely throw him, if she could. She raised her arms to shoulder height and started the slow shimmer she had learnt from Moroccan belly dancers. Slow was always more difficult than fast. It took masterly control.

He was quick to catch on, swaying his body in a complementary pattern while he wove his hands through movements that captured the essence of Eastern dancing. His eyes held hers, mesmerising in their intent, forcing her to acknowledge he had matched her.

She switched to jazz steps she had picked up in New Orleans. He was instantly on his toes, loose-limbed, lithe and dangerous, stalking her every move, pivoting, lunging, inventing an increasingly provocative reply to everything she initiated.

He didn't touch her, but Keira was aware that he was deliberately heightening the sexual element. His body language became more and more aggressive, and the hot challenge in his eyes goaded her to remain tantalisingly elusive, exulting in the teasing game and so intensely caught up in it that the ring of spectators applauding their performance barely impinged on her consciousness.

Suddenly he caught her to him. "Let's try some dirty dancing," he murmured, his powerful thighs thrusting hers into an intimate sequence of intricate steps, one strong arm keeping her body pinned to his, searing her with his animal heat.

"You said you would follow," she reminded him.

"I warned you I break rules."

He arched her back over his arm, pressing her lower body into his, making her aware that he was very much an aroused male intent on satisfaction.

"You go too far," she said breathlessly as he swung her up again and whirled her through a dizzying number of pirouettes that necessitated a fast juxtaposition of their legs.

"You incited it," he retorted. "Tell me your name."

It was on the tip of her tongue to say Keira when she caught sight of Justin watching them. Shame burned through her as she realised she had completely forgotten her cousin and his crisis. "We have to stop," she gasped, feeling her control slipping as the body directing hers asserted more and more dominance over what was happening.

"Tell me your name first," he insisted.

"Delilah," she choked out, hating having to use the alias Justin had demanded, but a promise was a promise. "Delilah O'Neil. And you must stop now. This has gone too far."

"Not nearly far enough," he murmured in her ear as he whirled her around one last time. "You know it. I know it. Why stop?"

"I came here with someone else. I must go back to him."

"Make your excuses. Leave him. Come with me."

"I don't even know your name."

"Nick Sarazin."

"Then please, Nick. I owe my companion loyalty."

His eyes blazed their command into hers, but Keira believed in loyalty. He might have captivated her body, but not her will. She was far too conscious of Justin's need to callously ignore it. If Nick Sarazin was truly attracted to her, he would make another time and place for them to meet.

Frustration momentarily tightened his face and hardened his eyes. "Very well," he said, bringing their dance to an abrupt but graceful halt. "Go back to him. When you change your mind I'll still be here, waiting for you."

The arrogant assumption pricked her pride. She stepped back from him, her green eyes meeting his in cool challenge. "I think, Mr. Sarazin, you've had your own way with women far too easily for far too long.

Wait, by all means, but *I* shall not come to you. If you want me, you'll have to find me. Thank you for the dance.''

The surprise on his face was intensely satisfying to Keira. She smiled at him, then swung on her heel and headed towards Justin, who was still standing where she had seen him.

Very conscious of having wavered off the plan, Keira quickly wiped off her smile and constructed an apologetic expression. It was difficult. She could feel the blue eyes of Nick Sarazin boring into her like laser beams. She couldn't resist swinging her bottom, which was now free of its cramped ache.

Nick Sarazin was the one, all right. Keira still felt his heat in her blood, like an intoxicant or a fever. But falling in love was a serious business. Nick Sarazin had to be taught that. Keira did not intend to be taken lightly. To her mind, there was a proper way of going about things, and while she loved spontaneity, she strongly disliked rude disregard for other people's feelings. There had to be giving as well as taking.

It was not as if Justin was some casual escort who meant nothing to her. Justin was family. Not that Nick Sarazin knew that, but he hadn't bothered to find out, either. He simply hadn't cared about anything except having his own way with her. His self-assurance definitely needed dinting. A bit.

Oddly, Justin wasn't looking at her at all. His gaze was fixed on a point over her shoulder, and far from appearing vexed or in any way upset, he was projecting a nonchalant confidence. He gave her a warm smile of approval as she joined him.

"Marvellous dancing, Delilah. You seem to have met your match," he remarked while handing her the drink he had been holding for her.

"Thanks, Justin." She looked at him quizzically. "You don't mind?"

"Not at all. I think I'll have to learn how to dance like that."

She frowned. "I meant about him. He, uh, kind of carried me off."

A sly little smile tilted her cousin's mouth. "He looked as though he wanted to do a lot more than that."

Keira flushed. "Well, the truth of the matter is he fancies me."

"And do you fancy him?"

"Yes, I do," she confessed. "Rather a lot. But I won't let you down, Justin."

"Oh, don't let me stop you from following your heart's desire."

She looked at him incredulously. Such generosity of spirit from Justin, against his own interests, didn't seem like him at all. Keira wondered if he'd been sinking more drinks than was good for him, but he didn't seem to be at all pie-eyed.

"What about your plan?" she reminded him.

Sheer unholy triumph glittered in his eyes. "The plan, my dear Delilah, is working perfectly. You already have my eternal gratitude. Louise doesn't know what to think. The mat has been whipped out from under her feet. The tables are already turned. Just look at me adoringly for a few moments."

Keira tried to oblige but it was difficult. She felt very confused. "I don't understand, Justin," she said as she did her best to adjust her body language to express what she didn't feel for her cousin. "What about the man you want seduced?"

"The natural order of things is now in progress. You don't have to worry about it."

Keira breathed a sigh of relief.

Justin's eyes narrowed. "In fact, I now suspect that Louise was using him as camouflage to get me to change my mind."

"About what?"

He gave her a stern look. "That is our private business. But the plot gets thicker and thicker, the intrigues deeper and deeper. Louise can be a very tricky fighter, but she's met her match in me. Oh yes! I'm more than a match for my wife!"

He paused to savour that thought, then beamed happily at Keira. "What we can be sure of, at this point in time, is that I'm winning. And winning well. Which is the main thing."

Keira sighed. She was sure she could be a lot more helpful to Justin if only he'd tell her what was going on. Apart from which, now that she had Justin's permission, she very much wanted to follow her heart's desire. Except that course was not viable at the present moment. She had just spiked it with her retort to Nick's arrogance. She actually needed to stay with Justin to force Nick Sarazin into an appraisal of his manners and expectations.

Consoling herself with the thought that at least she didn't have to pretend an interest in some other man,

Keira resigned herself to a continuation of the Delilah role. "So what's next on the menu, field marshal?" she asked, hoping to get a glimmer of what was in Justin's mind.

"Just keep projecting adoration," he said smugly. "You do it very well."

"Thank you. But I'm not too sure my heart's desire is going to like that, Justin. I don't want to put him off."

Her cousin gave her a wise look. "Trust me. That's precisely what will make him even more determined to take you away from me. I promise you he'll make another move before the night is out."

"Why do you think that?" Keira asked, hoping it was true.

"Instinct." He grinned. "And the way he watched you come to me. The fire is alight. We have to keep it burning. So we'll walk slowly across the floor, ignoring everyone else, totally immersed in our love for each other."

He tucked her arm around his and looked fatuously at her. They walked...slowly...and Keira did her best to follow Justin's lead. She examined her cousin's eyes as she had never examined them before. They were a nice brown but she found herself craving blue. Besides which, she wasn't absolutely sure Justin was right about this. She didn't want Nick Sarazin to start thinking she was seriously attached to Justin. On the other hand, that hadn't stopped him from approaching her in the first place.

All the same, Keira couldn't help feeling that feeding a fire was a very dangerous thing to do. Fires could get out of control. Fires could destroy. She had a strong urge to back off.

"This is getting to be a bit of a strain, Justin," she warned him. "I don't know how long I can keep it up."

"Not much longer, Keira."

"You forgot to call me Delilah."

"Damn! Delilah, Delilah, Delilah. I never was good with names."

"That's because they're not numbers."

"Which reminds me, you didn't slip up with your dancing partner, did you? You told him you were Delilah O'Neil?"

"Yes. But I didn't like it, Justin. I might get serious with Nick Sarazin."

"No problem," Justin pontificated. "If it doesn't get serious it won't matter what your name is. It it does get serious, he won't care about such a triviality. Take my word for it. A man doesn't care about names. It's the woman that counts."

"Is that how you feel about Louise?"

His fatuous look tightened into grim determination. "I wouldn't have married Louise if she wasn't the woman for me. The only woman. And by God, she's going to stay my woman!"

No doubt about it, Justin felt very deeply about Louise. Keira hoped Louise felt the same way about him and that their differences would soon be sorted out. She very much wanted to get on with her own life and she fiercely hoped Nick Sarazin would be part of it. A big part.

"You must stay Delilah O'Neil until I tell you everything's okay," Justin commanded.

Keira sighed compliance. "As you wish, field marshal." She couldn't very well upset his plan if it *was* actually working, but if his judgement was wrong... Keira shook her head. That didn't bear thinking about.

"Now we shall circle the room and make a spectacle of ourselves," he instructed. "Show the world that Justin Rigby Brooks need never have any trouble with women."

"Are you sure this is not going over the top, Justin?" Keira demanded critically.

"Think of the loan you need from me," he reminded her.

He did have a point.

Keira managed a fair show of adoration for about ten minutes, but the strain was getting to her facial muscles. She desperately needed a break so she excused herself to go to the powder room. Justin didn't mind giving her this consideration and pointed her down a hallway to the bedroom at the end of it, which, he said, had an en suite bathroom.

There were two women touching up their make-up in front of the dressing-table mirror in the bedroom. They assured Keira that the bathroom was free. Keira dallied in the bathroom for a while. She was beginning to feel very tired. Jet lag catching up fast, she thought, and splashed water over her face in an attempt to keep the draining fatigue at bay for a little while longer.

She desperately hoped she hadn't put Nick Sarazin off with all this adoration aimed at Justin. Yet if her cousin was any yardstick about how a man felt about the right woman, Nick Sarazin would find a way to win her, no matter what. If he truly did think they were made for each other.

When Keira emerged from the bathroom, a slim dark-haired woman was pacing the bedroom floor in tense agitation. Keira instantly felt a twinge of guilt for having dallied so long. The woman looked quite distressed.

Keira made an apologetic gesture. "Sorry..."

If looks could kill, she would have been reduced to dust on the spot. Dark brown eyes stabbed violent murder as the woman spoke in bitter accusation.

"Just what do you think you're doing with my husband, you... you brazen hussy?"

CHAPTER THREE

KEIRA'S INITIAL SHOCK from the verbal attack faded into the realisation that this woman surely had to be Louise. Justin's wife of four years—a wife who had walked out on him for reasons unknown—a wife who had flaunted another man under Justin's nose.

A curious fascination gripped Keira as she appraised her wayward cousin-in-law. Louise had a neat professional look about her. Justin would like that, Keira realised. Her thick black hair was cut into a short stylish bob that suited her round face. It was a pretty face, dominated by large dark eyes flashing jealous fury at Keira.

She was short and petite, and Justin would like that, too. It would make him feel very manly and protective. She wore a yellow silk dress with black polka dots and a fancy black patent leather belt. The effect was smart more than sexy, but there was certainly no doubting the curvaceous femininity of Louise's figure.

Whatever the bone of contention that ruptured their relationship, it was apparent Justin had succeeded in lighting an extremely passionate fire in his wife. She was certainly not indifferent to him. Which meant their marriage could be saved, given the right help.

However, saving a marriage was very tricky business. The utmost tact was called for. When all the problems were resolved, Keira wanted to be friends with Justin's wife, so her first priority was to defuse the violent enmity that was presently aimed at her.

She offered an open, friendly smile. "Are you Louise?"

It provoked violent rejection. "You sly bitch! You know exactly who I am."

Keira tried sweet reason. "How can I? We've never met before."

"Don't act the dumb blonde with me or I'll tear the skin off your face!" Louise sniped viciously. "I know you're not dumb."

"No, I'm not dumb. But I do feel rather at sea with this situation," Keira said soothingly. "If you care about your husband, why did you leave him?"

Louise moved so fast Keira didn't see the hand coming. It hit her a ringing blow across the face. "How dare you think you can interfere with my marriage! Mind your own damned business!"

Keira dazedly lifted a hand to her stinging cheek. She had never been physically struck in her whole life. She abhorred violence of any kind. Yet, in a way, she couldn't blame Louise for being upset, considering the provocation Justin had masterminded. Keira began to suspect there would be repercussions when Louise found out who the brazen hussy really was, and how she had been tricked.

One thing was certain. She could hardly fight with Louise, and she didn't want to. She edged warily away. Louise seemed to be working herself up for another

assault. Keira tried to present a logical point of view
for her cousin-in-law's more sober consideration.

"If you leave a husband, it implies you don't want
him any more. That makes him fair game for other
women," she said pertinently.

"You dirty, devious witch! He's not fair game!"
Louise shrieked. "He's mine!"

Perhaps not the right time for logic, Keira thought,
but decided it might be worthwhile to push one more
point. "Then don't you think you should do something about keeping him?" she advised, backing farther away as Louise advanced on her.

She saw the doorway out of the corner of her eye.
Keira decided this was Justin's problem, not hers, and
she was better off out of it. If she could make her escape until the madness of this situation was resolved...

"You sneaky, wicked slut!" Louise screamed.

"I'm not!" Keira defended.

"If you don't keep your eyes off my husband, I'll
tear them out!"

"There's no need for that," Keira said hastily.
"There is an explanation...."

That seemed to inflame Louise even further. "I'll
give you an explanation! Written in blood on your
face!" Her hands were lifting like talons. She meant
it.

Keira backtracked fast. "I'm fond of Justin," she
said defensively. "But that's all. You see—"

Louise sprang at her, bloody murder glittering in her
eyes. Keira turned and ran. She was out of the bedroom and a couple of steps down the hallway when her

hair was caught from behind. The yank nearly took her head off. I'm going to be scalped, she thought.

"Justin!" she yelled, needing him to get here on the run. A very fast run. He had a lot of quick explaining to do to douse this fire. He *had* gone too far. Things were totally out of control. And she was the one about to be destroyed!

"Hussy!" Louise screamed, pulling on Keira's hair so that she was dragged around to face Louise.

Keira could see the satisfaction and triumph in Louise's eyes as she disentangled one hand and raised it to claw down her face. Keira threw up an arm to defend herself and cried out again, more desperately.

"Justin, Justin, Justin!"

Louise's hand slashed down. It didn't reach Keira's face. It was arrested only millimetres from striking. Thank God Justin had got here, Keira thought in shaky relief. But it wasn't Justin.

"Oh, I say!" came a very British voice as a big brawny arm swept between the two women, forcibly separating them, giving Keira some much-needed room away from Louise.

Keira drew back her head as Louise's fingers loosened from her hair. She looked up gratefully to her rescuer. Her eyes met a walrus moustache and she stared in startled surprise at the big retired wrestler who had sat next to her on the plane.

"Surely there has to be a better way," he started to chide Louise, but got no further.

Louise turned on the instant, her black fury switched to him. Keira had to hand it to Louise. She had fast reactions. Without so much as a pause she kneed him violently in the groin. The poor man didn't have time to look surprised. His face went white. He emitted a tortured groan of pain and doubled over.

Louise glared at Keira over the poor man's stricken body. "Keep away from my husband or you'll get worse than that! I'll kill you!" she threatened. Then she tossed her head in the air and marched off into an admiring crowd who politely clapped.

It must have looked like a David and Goliath contest, and little David, the underdog, had won. Keira instantly knew that everyone was going to be against her. She was cast in the role of the bad woman. The marriage breaker. I've done nothing, she wailed inwardly.

Two faces seemed to leap out at Keira from the mass of people in the immediate vicinity.

Justin, beaming absolute delight.

Nick Sarazin, looking darkly and doubly frustrated.

Then the heaving groans of the retired British wrestler demanded Keira's attention. She bent to help him, her hand sliding over his shoulders. "Are you all right?" she asked sympathetically.

"No," he moaned. "Not all right at all."

"I'll get you onto a bed," she suggested.

"Finished," he said. "I'm finished."

Keira saw action was imperative. She quickly tried the nearest door, found it opened to a bedroom, then urged the poor man towards it.

"You need rest," she told him comfortingly. "I'm so sorry you were hurt. Please tell me if there's anything I can do."

"Just finished." He tottered a couple of steps, saw the bed, looked at Keira in anguish. "I beg you, leave me. Please..."

"But there must be something..."

"No! No!" he cried, looking quite distressed. "There's nothing you can do. You—you're dangerous. Totally dangerous."

"No, I'm not," Keira assured him.

"Please. Leave me. I'll be all right. Just finished."

"Nothing more can happen to you," Keira promised.

"Go away!" he begged. "I don't want to be beaten up by some jealous husband. Go away."

Oh, dear! Another nasty incident, Keira thought. "If you're sure..." she said uncertainly.

"Yes, yes," he urged desperately. "Never been more sure. Leave me alone with my pain."

"I'm sorry," she said, and saw relief pass over his face as she backed away. He lurched into the bedroom and shut the door behind him.

Keira heaved a deep sigh. Just because things seemed to happen around her, it wasn't all her fault, was it? He had spilled the coffee all by himself this morning. And tonight... Well, it had been his choice to be the gallant gentleman. For which Keira was truly grateful. She should have thanked him. Somehow she didn't think he would appreciate her thanks right now, so she decided it was better not to press the matter. Perhaps she would do so if she ever ran into him again.

Keira wondered what he was doing here. It seemed an odd coincidence that both of them should have come to the same house on their first night in Sydney. But it was a small world, she reflected, shrugging off any further speculation. The retired British wrestler was irrelevant to the immediate problem.

One thing had been made very clear. Louise was far from indifferent to Justin. And she certainly wasn't indifferent to Keira. Passions were running very deep here, and it was time to wipe that smug look off her cousin's face. Fighting fire with fire had elements of extreme danger, and Keira passionately hoped Justin knew how to put the fire out. Otherwise Louise was going to make life very difficult for Keira in the future.

Apart from which, Keira felt very unhappy about Nick Sarazin having witnessed that nasty little scene. Somehow it made all her role-playing with Justin seem sordid. She was not a marriage breaker. She had been doing her best to be a marriage saver. But it hadn't looked that way. If Justin's strategy had lost her a chance with Nick Sarazin... A lump of lead dragged at Keira's heart. It didn't bear thinking about.

She braced herself for the fray and made her way through the crowd to Justin, who was looking far too cocky for his own good. He needed to be brought down to earth with a good thump.

"This job as a private soldier is finished, Justin," she said. "That's the end!"

"Ah... Delilah, Delilah, Delilah, I adore you," he crooned sickeningly. Then grinned. "Great little fighter, my wife. As feisty as they come. She was going to kill you. Sorry about your hair, but it does demonstrate how much Louise has been kidding me. Everything is going marvellously well.''

"It's finished!'' Keira repeated emphatically. "You tell Louise the truth.''

"Never.''

"Then I'll tell her!''

He frowned at the determined defiance flashing from her green eyes. "Be serious, Keira.''

"I am serious. Deadly serious. I am not going to die for your honour or glory or happiness, Justin.''

"Look,'' he said appeasingly, "there's more to this than meets the eye.''

"Then you'd better start explaining it to me,'' Keira demanded, taking a very firm stand.

"Not here. It'll spoil everything. Just hang in a little while longer.''

"No.''

"Until tomorrow.''

"No.''

"A few hours more.''

"No.''

"I'll double the loan. And I won't demand payment of any interest on the money.''

Keira could hardly believe her ears. She had never known her cousin to be so free with his money. Except when he had sent her the airfare to come to his wedding. Which she had missed. He must be absolutely convinced that this plan of his was going to save his marriage. But Keira had her doubts. Serious ones, at that!

"I'll triple the loan to keep the plan strictly between us until tomorrow,'' Justin pressed keenly.

Keira frowned hard at him. She had no need for that much money. All she had wanted from him was a reasonable loan to tide her over until she could get a job. Money was not that important to her. Not as it was to Justin. Either he was completely nuts or he was desperate for her not to interfere in what was, when all was said and done, *his* marriage and *his* private business. She just hoped he knew what he was doing.

"All right," she conceded reluctantly. "But not for love nor money will I be persuaded to let you use me falsely beyond that, Justin. And I'm not going home with you tonight. I won't have Louise thinking I'm committing adultery with her husband. You've got to tell her the truth about me pretty darned quick or you won't have a marriage to save."

"I will. As soon as I get the right opportunity."

"Promise!"

"I promise. In the meantime, I take your point about spending the night with me, so what are we going to do with you?"

"A room in a hotel."

"Okay."

"A suite."

"What do you need a suite for?"

"Bodily comfort. After all I've been through—"

"Suites are expensive."

"Consider it danger money. And proof of how eternally grateful you are."

She had him over a barrel. He conceded handsomely. "Whatever you want. But you've got to stay Delilah until tomorrow."

"The sooner you tell Louise the better, Justin," she warned. "I'm going to find a telephone right now and book a nice big safe suite for my well-being. And I'm going to stay there until you've cleared my name with Louise. You owe me that."

The cost of maintaining her in a suite should clear his mind about when to tell his wife the truth, Keira reasoned. Having thrown down her ultimatum, she marched off in search of a telephone, determined to hold Justin to his promise.

Nick Sarazin found her first.

All of a sudden he was in front of her, blocking her way, his blue eyes flashing a hard challenge. "He's no good for you, Delilah," he stated with firm conviction. "If you didn't know before, you know now. He's married."

It was one thing getting Justin to sort out the problem with Louise. Nick Sarazin was a completely different kettle of fish. Keira owed him nothing, and his demanding manner got under her skin, scraping over her recently lacerated pride. Not only that, he was making assumptions that he had no right to make.

"Justin has been very good to me," Keira said loftily. "So you don't have anything to worry about. And I happen to be rather fond of him." Which was the truth. She *was* rather fond of Justin, although after what had happened with Louise, that fondness was rapidly diminishing.

Nick Sarazin's jaw line tightened. It made him look very aggressive, like a warrior about to fight to his death. The blue eyes glittered with repressed anger.

"You were well named Delilah," he grated. "Very accurately named."

Keira found her pulse beating faster. Nick Sarazin had definitely got the wrong idea about her. She wondered how she could correct this misinterpretation. She couldn't very well reveal what she had assured Justin she would not reveal. But her sense of loyalty was wearing perilously thin.

Although Justin had been right about Nick.

He had made another move on her, and he was certainly burning.

Her cousin had next to no understanding of women, but it did seem he had an understanding of what went on in men's minds.

Once again, Keira tried to soothe troubled waters. "I guess my family had reasons for bestowing that particular name on me, just as your family had reasons for bestowing yours on you," she said reasonably. "You have to live with yours, with its satanic overtones, just as I have to live with mine."

"Are you always so callous to other people?" he demanded, his sympathies obviously with Louise.

Keira's chin lifted. Her green eyes held his in cool challenge, refusing to give him any quarter whatsoever, not on the grounds he had raised.

"No," she stated flatly. "Most of the time I'm just me. If you don't like that, Mr. Sarazin, just step out of my way and let me get on with my own business. After all, it's you interfering with me, not the other way around."

His hands shot out and gripped her wrists, determined that she stay...at least until he had finished with her. Another liberty, Keira thought, but since she didn't mind, she didn't say anything. She liked him holding her and was glad that he wanted to, but she was not about to take any disparagement from him.

"What do you find so attractive about him?" he demanded to know. "Dammit! You can't find him attractive!"

Keira had to admit to herself she didn't find Justin all that attractive, but she certainly wasn't going to admit that to a stranger. Family was family. She searched her mind for a reply and found one she thought suitable.

"He's the kind of man who always takes care of me once he gives me a commitment. It's a quality I value. Perhaps you'd like to tell me your rating on that, Mr. Sarazin," she invited mockingly.

"I could give you more love in a minute than you'd ever get from him in a lifetime," he retorted fiercely, his voice throbbing with raw passion, his eyes searing the coolness from hers. He looked hard at her, hotly assessing. "Make that time factor *one hour.*"

Keira's heart flipped over. Once again she felt a fierce tug on her soul, and a treacherous excitement flooded her veins. The thought of experiencing his promise almost eroded all common sense, yet a thread of sanity insisted this might be a line he threw at all women.

"You really believe you can deliver on that?" she asked doubtfully.

His hands left her wrists and started sliding around her waist. He moved closer, deliberately heightening his physical impact on her. His eyes simmered with memories of the more intimate contact they had already shared with his brand of "dirty dancing."

"Certain," he said with absolute conviction.

"Maybe we only dance well together," she suggested defensively, refusing to admit the chaos he wrought inside her.

"We're compatible," he said gruffly.

"You don't like me," she protested.

"What has liking to do with passion?"

"You feel passion?"

"Very definitely." His eyes burned into hers as he spoke in a low intense voice. "I want your hair on my pillow. I want to bury my face in it. I want to ravish your mouth and know all its dark inner secrets. I want your body entwined around mine in the most primitive dance of all. I want your wild earthy rhythm pulsing through me. And I promise I'll take you where you've never been before. We were made for each other, Delilah."

It was as if his words had a life of their own, writhing through her in seductive temptation, stealing her breath, squeezing her heart, knotting her stomach, sending quivers of weakness down her legs, tingles through her toes. What woman in her right mind could resist such an offer?

Was this how it was—a want, a need, a desire that overrode everything else? But what about trust and caring and loving—weren't they more important? Why did she feel that he was the one? Was there any real choice, or was it all preordained through some physical chemistry neither she nor he had any control over?

She suddenly felt a strong empathy for the passion that had driven Louise to such violence. It ran through Keira's mind in a wave of almost unbelievable ferocity that if Nick Sarazin took her and walked away, she would want to kill him. Yet not to experience what he offered her was another kind of death, a rejection of what could be.

"I want you," he said. "I want you to walk away from him right now. Forever. And come with me."

Somehow Keira found voice enough to ask, "Why are you so impetuous? Let's give it some time. I'll think about it."

"No time. No thinking. Now or never, Delilah. It's as simple as that. Make your choice."

The tension emanating from him tore along Keira's nerves. Nick Sarazin was not a conventional man. He was gambling the lot on one throw, and demanding that she do the same.

Keira wasn't afraid of taking risks. She had never been interested in a safe life. Safe meant limited and she refused to be limited to anything. Nevertheless, she was not rash and not about to take a leap into the unknown.

"Where are we going?"

His eyes glinted with satisfaction. He relaxed enough to smile, sensing his victory. "Away from Sydney. Away from everything. You can choose wherever you want. But we're going."

Oh, dear, Keira thought. He was going to make it difficult for her to exert any control over this particular outcome. What was bound to happen was almost inevitable. Did he view relationships in terms of easy come, easy go? she wondered. On the other hand, perhaps she would be able to convince him that he didn't want to let her go. Ever. The fact that he hadn't wanted to let her go tonight, despite all that had happened, gave Keira some reassurance that there was a chance of a future with him.

"The beach house?" she suggested. After the cold of Iceland and Europe, she really fancied some hot Australian sun. If he gave her time to enjoy it.

"Fine!"

He scooped her hard against him, and before Keira could have any second thoughts about her decision, he was pushing through the crowd towards the front door, sweeping her along with him.

"Nick, I have to speak to Justin first," she protested.

"No. He's married. You don't owe him any loyalty and you don't speak to him again."

"You're putting demands on me already. I don't like that, Nick."

"I'm saving you from yourself," he said grimly.

"But Justin's got my things."

"I'll buy you whatever you need."

"I don't want you buying me stuff. It would make me feel bought. I never like to feel bought. In fact, I resent it."

"Send for whatever you need tomorrow."

"Justin will worry about me."

"You can call him on my car phone."

"You'll listen in."

"Most certainly."

"Why can't I speak to him before we leave?"

"Because you're finished with him. Because you've made up your mind. Now stick to it, Delilah. Remember at all times that he doesn't count any more."

Jealous. And possessive. And so far he had nothing to be jealous and possessive about. Maybe he was just plain demanding. Yet there were very positive signals of passion, Keira thought, so she didn't protest too much.

"Haven't you ever heard of politeness, Mr. Sarazin?"

"Yes. And I've also heard of double-dealing."

Keira thought about that highly questionable remark as they went down the front steps to the driveway. "You don't trust me," she accused.

His eyes glittered mockingly in the semi-darkness. His face had taken on a satanic look. "Not one iota."

"You're well named, Nick."

He grinned wickedly. "So are you, Delilah."

"Devil!"

"Seductress!"

The irony of the situation suddenly descended upon Keira. She wasn't a Delilah, nor a seductress, nor a woman hankering after a married man! And twenty-four hours ago she had been sitting beside the retired British wrestler with the walrus moustache, unaware of Justin's crisis and unaware of Nick Sarazin's existence!

"I don't think this is going to work out," she said limply. There was too much misunderstanding at this early stage.

Nick paused in his step, looked at her, then hoisted her in his arms and clutched her tightly against his chest. "Just stay put," he commanded, "and let me worry about that."

He strode along the driveway as Keira tried to catch her breath. Her arms automatically found their way around his neck. It was a very strong neck. He was a very strong man. He made Keira feel very feminine.

"Why are you carrying me?" she asked huskily. Her voice was melting. Her brain told her she should be protesting very firmly. Nick Sarazin had no right to seize control like this, taking away her choices. But somehow the messages from her brain were getting quite muddled by a lot of strange and strong sensations.

"Because I feel like it," he said in a harsh, gravelly tone.

Keira decided she didn't really mind him taking this particular liberty. As long as he didn't make a habit of taking liberties without any consultation with her.

He didn't carry her far. A black two-seater Jaguar sports sedan was parked outside one of the garages at the side of the house. He reached the passenger door and let her feet slide to the ground, but she was still held fast in his embrace. She wasn't sure if it was his heart thumping so hard or hers, but when he lowered his head towards her upturned face, Keira felt an exultant leap of anticipation through her whole body.

Because of their heated exchange, she had expected him to kiss her with passion, yet his lips moulded slowly, sensually into the fullness of hers. He tasted them exquisitely, seducing them into opening farther and farther with an escalating range of exciting sensations.

Then he was exploring the full intimacy of her mouth, weaving erotic dances with his tongue, stirring dimensions of feeling that sent bursts of wonderment through Keira's brain. A hand stroked her long neck, wound its way through her hair, took hold, and suddenly there was an explosion of passion, a wild, plundering drive for total possession with a ravishing stream of kisses that came so hot and fast that Keira was barely aware of one ending before another began.

Waves of excitement flooded through her body, and it seemed that he absorbed the very essence of her so that she floated weightless, her legs a useless support, his arms supporting her, his body a hard solid raft in a shifting sea of turbulent sensation. So intense were the feelings he evoked that Keira moaned in bereft protest when he finally lifted his head away, leaving her with an unforgettable imprint of the kind of loving he was capable of giving her.

And he was far from unaffected. He was as aroused as she was, breathing hard and fast as he lifted his hand to cup her face. He stroked his thumb lightly over her tingling lips as his eyes glittered into hers, piercing the daze of mindless wanting.

"Remember that when you speak to Justin Brooks," he commanded in a harsh rasp.

Then he unlocked the car door, opened it and eased her onto the low-slung passenger seat. Keira could barely think, let alone comprehend what had just happened to her. If that was a minute or two...what would an hour of Nick Sarazin's loving be like?

Her limbs were like water. It didn't occur to her to fasten her seat belt. Nick did it for her. Then he was beside her in the driver's seat. The powerful engine of the sports car throbbed into life. They shot down the driveway, out into the street and away from the party.

Nick punched out some numbers on the car phone, picked up the receiver and told whoever answered to take care of the house, look after the colonel's needs, he would be back in a fortnight or so, and he wanted to speak to Justin Brooks, who was one of the guests. Then he handed the receiver to Keira.

The blue eyes bored into her, hard, hot and demanding. "Tell him you're with me. You're finished with him and you're staying with me. Permanently."

CHAPTER FOUR

PERMANENTLY?

A wild rush of elation danced through Keira's brain. Nick must think she was the one for him!

Then a niggling little voice whispered this might only be an emphatic expression to drive home the point that Justin was to have no more relevance in her life. Which, of course, she couldn't agree to at all. Justin was family.

Besides which, Nick had no right to order her around. He didn't own her. He had no claim to exclusive rights on her, either. They weren't married yet.

That last thought gave Keira pause for consideration. Was she going to marry him if he asked her? It might be very difficult to settle down to a humdrum existence after all her footloose years. On the other hand, she couldn't imagine Nick Sarazin leading a humdrum life. And she couldn't imagine wanting any other man but him.

All the same, he was not going to order her around. He was going to have to temper this demanding habit if he wanted to be her husband. It was not a quality she valued. In fact, it was decidedly negative to her way of thinking. Taking care of her was fine, but taking care of her against her will was definitely a no-no.

"Justin Brooks." Her cousin's voice.

Keira took a deep breath. Nick was listening. She had to get this right to avoid any more misunderstandings that she couldn't explain away.

"Justin, this is Delilah. I've taken off with Nick Sarazin. You might remember him. He's the man I danced with. So you don't have to worry about me any more. I'm calling you from his car phone and we're on our way to..."

She looked questioningly at Nick. "Where is your beach house?"

Blue eyes locked with green. "I don't want him coming after you."

Keira sighed. If only she could tell him the truth, she could dispel that notion in a second, but... She spoke into the phone. "Justin... Nick doesn't want you coming after me. You won't do that, will you? Tell him that whatever Delilah decides is fine by you. I'm passing the receiver to him."

She held it to Nick's ear and they both heard Justin give firm assurance that Delilah had his every blessing to live her life as she saw fit. She smiled triumphantly at Nick and resumed her conversation with her cousin.

"Thank you, Justin. I knew I could rely on you to say that. And I know I can rely on you to send my bags by special courier to... What's the address, Nick?"

He conceded it with a dark brooding look.

She passed it on and waited until Justin wrote it down. "I want them tomorrow, Justin. Without fail," she said firmly. "And I also need the payment you owe me, so please include that with my bags. I won't be happy if it's not there, Justin. In fact, I don't know what I'll do if it's not there."

"It'll be there," he promised. "And Delilah..." He said her name with pointed emphasis. "I understand that you're finished with our mutual project, and that's fine by me, but I've still some way to go, so the cat stays in the bag until tomorrow. Okay?"

She sighed in resignation. "Okay. Tomorrow. Goodbye and good luck, Justin."

"And the best of luck to you, too, Delilah," he said with uncharacteristic fervour. It must be because he's so grateful, Keira thought, because she had never known her cousin to be overly demonstrative with good wishes or affection.

She hung up with a feeling of deep satisfaction. The rift was definitely healed. Justin had forgiven her for taking off with the sheikh and missing his wedding. However, there was the difficulty with Louise to overcome before they could all be a happy family again. She hoped Justin's plan covered that because Keira didn't like being cast as the bad woman. She wasn't bad at all.

"What's on tomorrow?" Nick demanded suspiciously.

Keira threw him a vexed look. This not trusting her one iota was distinctly tiresome. "I'm getting my bags," she stated patiently. "And the money Justin owes me."

"I suppose you're used to twisting any man you like around your little finger," Nick remarked in a savage tone.

Keira's vexation with the situation deepened. *He* still thought she was bad. She hoped he wasn't going to be a slow learner about her character or she would run out of patience with him.

"I get the impression that *you're* used to twisting any woman you like around *your* little finger," she retorted, determined to give him tit for tat until he started to get reasonable.

His mocking smile had a grim edge. "But not you."

"I'm a free spirit," she said, which was a fair assessment of the truth.

She thought that the right man, if he used the right kind of rope, could tie her down, but she wasn't going to be bound or gagged if she didn't want it to happen. Nick Sarazin had to learn that, and he might as well start learning now.

"What did Justin Brooks owe you payment for?"

Keira threw him a look of reproof. "Just because I let you get away with listening in on a private conversation, it doesn't give you any right to know my private business. What I've done with my life up to this point in time is absolutely no business of yours. You'd do much better if you simply take me as you find me, and stop reading all sorts of nasty things into my words and actions."

She paused, then pointedly added, "I don't like it. In fact, it could wear out my passion pretty darned fast."

His mouth twitched into a conciliatory smile. "I beg your pardon. I was merely curious, not thinking nasty things about you." He raised an appealing eyebrow at her. "Am I not to know anything of your life?"

"That depends," she said cautiously. She was mollified by the smile, but she still had to watch her step because of Justin's plan.

"On what?" Nick asked.

"What you tell me about your life," Keira answered lightly.

"It's an open book. Ask away as much as you like," he invited.

"The house where the party was held, that's yours, too?"

"Yes. That's my Sydney residence."

Which made Nick the host of tonight's party. Therefore he must know Justin, if only as an acquaintance. And he probably knew Louise, as well. Since all three had some connection, social or business, Keira could understand why Justin wanted her to retain her alias with Nick until everything was settled.

"What was the party for?" she asked. "I mean, was there any special reason for it?"

He gave her a quizzical look, then shrugged. "It was in celebration of the successful launch of a new product."

"Something you make?" she asked curiously, wondering where all his opulence came from.

The quizzical look was slightly harder this time, blue eyes sharply probing hers. "Don't you know who I am, Delilah?"

She returned her own puzzlement. "How could I? I only met you tonight. You told me your name, but you didn't tell me anything else about yourself."

He frowned, as though not quite believing her. "And my name meant nothing to you?"

"No. Why should it?"

He shook his head. A self-mocking little smile played over his lips. "Why, indeed?" he murmured.

"Are you famous or something?" Keira asked.

He gave a dry chuckle. "Apparently not. Though I had imagined most people would have heard of me. I've run a high-profile business for a fair number of years."

"What kind of business?"

He grinned knowingly. "Advertising. The Sarazin Advertising Agency."

He said it as though that had to mean something to her. But it didn't. "Well, it's nice for you it's been so successful," she said.

He looked incredulously at her. "You can't mean you've never heard of that, either?"

She shrugged apologetically. "Sorry."

He simply couldn't accept it. "Don't you ever watch television?"

"Not much. I travel a lot."

"Where?"

"All over."

"All over what?"

"All over the world. I've been out of Australia for a number of years," she explained. "And before then...well, I was in out-of-the-way places. Television wasn't important."

This time he looked at her with sharp curiosity. "What *was* important?"

"Oh, seeing things. Finding out things. Meeting people. Talking to them." She smiled. "Call it a long journey of discovery."

His eyes lingered appreciatively on her smile for several seconds before he turned his gaze back to the road. Then he slowly shook his head, a bemused expression on his face.

"You must have done some travelling, too," she remarked.

"Why do you say that?"

"Few people would pick up that kind of Eastern dancing unless they've experienced it first-hand."

He nodded. "I knocked around the world for a couple of years when I was younger."

"How old are you now?"

"Thirty-three. And you?"

"Twenty-six."

"What kind of job do you hold?"

She laughed. "I don't hold any kind of job for long. I move on, you see. I guess you could call me a Jill of all trades. A rolling stone. I've been everything from a shoe sales person to a hair model for shampoo. I was even nanny to a sheikh's son for a while."

"A sheikh," he repeated in dry amusement.

"Mmm, in Morocco. Very educational. I once thought being an archaeologist would be the most exciting job in the world, but it's not, you know. A lot of hard grind for very little reward."

"Where did you do your archaeology?"

"In Egypt. It wasn't a successful dig but it was an experience. I learnt a lot about Egypt."

"What has been your most exciting job?" he asked curiously.

She yawned. She couldn't help herself. Fatigue was washing over her in an overwhelming tide. She had only had short snatches of sleep in the last forty-eight hours. Even today, although she had spent several hours on a very comfortable bed, she hadn't had a long, restful sleep. Her biological clock was totally out of whack.

"I don't know that I could pick out a most exciting one," she replied, too weary to really think about it.

"Being a model?" he suggested.

"That was very boring. Good money, though."

"Not enough to keep you in it?"

"I had other things to do." She yawned again. "I'm sorry, Nick. I'm dreadfully tired. Would you mind very much if I dozed while you drive?"

"Go right ahead. There's a knob to the left of your seat if you want to lower the back rest," he said, flashing her a kindly smile.

"Thanks."

He was heart-wrenchingly handsome when he smiled like that, Keira thought. She adjusted the back rest and nestled herself into a more relaxed position. She closed her eyes and felt very content to be with him, not caring where they went, or how long it took them, as long as it was together.

"One last question, Delilah," he said softly.

"Mmm?" She didn't bother opening her eyes. Her lids felt very heavy.

"Do you do this kind of thing very often?"

"What?" Her mind was getting foggy.

"Take off with a man you don't know."

"Never before."

"Why are you doing it this time?" he asked her sharply.

She stirred herself enough to answer him, but her thoughts were drifting into a deeper haze. "You're the one...."

"The one...what?"

"King tide..."

"I don't understand."

It's very simple, she thought, but the words didn't reach her lips. They were lost as sleep overtook her, dragging her into dark oblivion.

Nick Sarazin glared at her in deep and mounting frustration. Who the hell was she? What was she? Where had she come from? What did she know? Who had sent her?

Her last words were utter gibberish, yet they had to have some meaning. She was certainly intelligent. As well as being so damned beautiful and alluring that he had been on fire for her from the moment he had seen her dancing.

A Delilah who had seduced her way around the world? So many question marks she raised.

Yet her face in sleep was as smooth and as innocent as a babe's.

And that hair! Was it real? He shifted uncomfortably in his seat. Just the thought of it made him stir. Everything about her made him feel more aroused than he could ever remember, as if somehow she embodied all that a woman should be or could be....

A fantasy, he thought mockingly. That was what she was. A siren from mythical legends. Green eyes like the sea. Maybe those words, king tide, did have some relevance. And if he didn't watch himself, he could drown in it. On the other hand, that might not be a bad fate.

The image of a mermaid swam into his mind. Ridiculous...absurd. He glanced at her long shapely legs. The loveliest legs he had ever seen. The way she could move them—the speed, the grace, the command—the sheer provocative sensuality of her body.

He'd got her. That was the main thing. Yet the question continued to tease his mind—what exactly had he got? The speculation began to irritate him and he leaned forward to switch the radio on. A Mozart concerto. He turned the volume low so as not to wake her.

From his Sydney home at Hunter's Hill, it was barely a two-hour trip to Forrester's Beach on the Central Coast. He liked the house he had bought there. It was simple. Comfortable but unpretentious, suitable for casual living. Of course, he had it serviced, but it didn't require live-in staff, and it gave him a sense of privacy, something that was becoming more and more precious to him these days. Once he had hankered after fame and wealth, but having achieved both, there was a price to pay. Nevertheless, having enjoyed economic freedom for years now, he would never want to give that up.

A free spirit. He looked at her face again. In some ways it was a strong face. Unusual bones, more delineated than most. Smoky eyelashes. How were they that colour if her hair was real? Yet how could a hairdresser achieve the variations of shade between white and deep gold? She was a strange contradictory creature.

Not many women defied him these days. Or challenged him, as she had. No fawning or flattery from her. He was beginning to believe that what he had achieved was totally meaningless to her. It had been a long, long time since he had felt uncertain of a conquest, and even now he wasn't sure she was a conquest. *A free spirit...*

But she would be his.

He'd make her his.

She was still fast asleep when he brought the car to a quiet halt in the driveway of the beach house. He alighted quietly, unlocked the house, switched on lights as he strode through it to the main bedroom. There he opened the sliding glass doors to let in fresh air and the sound of the ocean with its endless rolling surf. She would probably feel at home with that, he thought whimsically.

The sweet haunting scent of frangipani blooms wafted on the sea-breeze. An image floated into his mind. The soft velvet of fragrant petals shading from white through cream to deep gold. It brought a sensual smile to his lips.

He went to the linen cupboard, took out a sheet, walked quickly to the veranda and spread it on the double sun lounger. He leaned over the veranda railing and gathered as many blooms as he could reach from the huge frangipani tree that graced the north side of the house. He sprinkled the blooms over the sheet. All the elements, he thought, water, air, earth and the fire burning between them. It gave him a deeply primitive satisfaction in his arrangements.

He took one small spray of flowers with him to the kitchen where he paused long enough to put the kettle on to boil. Coffee seemed like a good idea. He wanted her awake, alert and responsive. Apart from needing his desire for her satisfied, Nick felt a sense of urgency about getting rid of that elusive quality Delilah O'Neil emanated. He wouldn't feel content until he had her precisely where he wanted her... in his arms, joined to him.

He returned to the car. She hadn't stirred. He opened her door, leaned down to unfasten her seat belt. His hand brushed over the soft fullness of her breast, lingered a moment, then dropped to the seat belt buckle. He wanted to touch her, but he wanted her knowing he was touching her.

Keira was awakened by an arm sliding under her legs and another burrowing around her shoulders. She opened her eyes, saw the darkly handsome face hovering over hers. The recognition in her heart was instant and electric. She smiled at her man.

"Are we there?" she asked.

"Yes," he said gruffly, and lifted her out of the car.

Keira wound her arms around his neck and nestled her head onto his broad shoulder. She breathed in the strong male scent of him and sighed in happy contentment.

Nick pushed the car door shut behind him and headed for the house.

Keira could hear the dull roar of the ocean, and there was a smell of salt in the air. The Pacific Ocean, she thought, half a world away from the Atlantic. She was home...home in many senses. It felt so right to have Nick Sarazin holding her like this.

He carried her through the house to a very large bedroom before setting her on her feet. His lips brushed over hers with what felt like loving tenderness.

"Are you all right, Delilah?"

"Mmm..."

He trailed soft little kisses around her face. "I've put the kettle on to boil. I'll go and make us some coffee. Okay?"

She'd prefer him to keep kissing her, but he had had quite a long drive and probably craved a cup of coffee. "Okay," she agreed.

He lifted a hand to her cheek and gently swept her hair from her face. She looked into his eyes, so vividly blue, enveloping her in their intensity.

"There's an en suite bathroom through that door." He nodded towards it. "How do you like your coffee?"

"Black."

"Sugar?"

"No. Straight black, thank you."

He smiled as he stroked her cheek in a soft salute. "Don't go back to sleep on me."

"I won't," she promised. Her skin was still tingling from his touch, and the feel of his body had aroused hers out of its lethargy.

He moved away to a row of wall cupboards, opened a door, pulled out a drawer, withdrew a cellophane packet. "I keep a supply of *yukatas* for guests," he explained. "They're—"

"Japanese lounging robes. Evolved from samurai ceremonial garments," Keira finished for him, smiling at his surprise. She walked over to take the packet from him. "I did tell you I've done a lot of travelling, and a lot of learning. Thank you, Nick. It will be handy until I get my things."

"Keep it if you like," he offered.

The practicalities of the situation had snapped Keira out of her trance. She looked searchingly at Nick Sarazin. Had he really meant permanent? There was a wary reserve in his eyes, as though he was uncertain of her, or uncertain of her reactions.

"There's a supply of shower caps in the bathroom, if you want to make use of one," he added.

"Thank you." Her green eyes flashed with a sharp stab of inquiry. "You're well prepared...for your guests."

He shrugged and gave an offhand smile. "A matter of hospitality."

Convenient hospitality? she wondered. She had acted on instinct, choosing to come with him, but she suddenly felt very unsure about his feelings for her. How deep did his passion go?

She recollected his question to her and decided that this was an appropriate time to toss it back at him. "Do you do this kind of thing very often? Taking off with a woman you don't know?"

He met the challenge in her eyes with hard self-mockery. "No. Never with women I don't know. But then I've never met a woman like you, Delilah. You are...exceptional. Therefore, like you, I make an exception—for you." One eyebrow lifted in sardonic inquiry. "Is that what you wanted to hear?"

"Only if it's the truth."

He gave a soft little laugh. "Take my word for it. You'll never hear a truer truth."

A bubble of happiness lifted her doubts away and she burst into a smile. "I think you're exceptional, too, Nick. Very arrogant, too dominating, too demanding, but definitely exceptional."

The blue eyes danced with amusement. "How am I supposed to respond to being chastised and complimented in the same breath?"

"Oh, you've got a few things to learn about me, Nick Sarazin. In fact, you're going to have to be a very fast learner," she advised pertly.

"I intend to be," he promised . . . or threatened.

There was suddenly an aura of intense purpose about him, and Keira once again felt a sense of danger. She knew intuitively that this man could hurt her as no-one else could—deeply, irrevocably. Warning messages slid across her mind—passion, fire burning out of control. And fire could destroy.

"I think I'll take a shower," she said.

"I'll go and make the coffee," he said.

And so they separated . . . for a while.

But Keira knew what was coming, as surely as night followed day. Nick Sarazin was not about to hold back. In coming with him, and in responding to his kisses as she had, Keira knew that Nick had every reason to be complacent about her consent. He was not to know, and probably would never believe, that sharing a bed with a man was not a common feature of her life, despite her twenty-six years. In fact, it was extremely uncommon. Which was probably why she was beginning to feel intensely vulnerable about it.

The timing was far too premature in one sense, yet Keira didn't believe time would make any difference to how she felt about Nick Sarazin. This inner certainty that he was the one had to be acted upon. However, going too far too soon might be a mistake. She might end up getting very badly hurt. The problem was... how could she tell if she was the one for him?

CHAPTER FIVE

THE PLEASANT BEAT of warm water washed the lingering fatigue from Keira's body. As she dried herself with a soft fluffy towel, her gaze drifted around the well-appointed bathroom. A lot of home comforts here, she thought appreciatively. Luxury and every possible convenience, even to a hair dryer and a specially magnified make-up mirror attached to the tiled wall beside the vanity bench.

Keira thrust her arms into the loose sleeves of the *yukata*. The light cotton garment was a sea-green colour, splattered with a navy-blue twig-style pattern. Nice combination, she thought, as she wrapped it around her and tied the belt. Then she whipped off the shower cap and shook her hair loose. For a few moments she examined her reflection in the mirror, wondering why Nick thought she was exceptional.

She knew he found her hair attractive, but hair was only hair. He surely wouldn't break his personal rules for something as superficial as that. Of course, there was the physical attraction, which had been quite close to explosive when he had swept her into his "dirty dancing." Did he feel a sharper desire for her than he'd felt for any other woman? Was it all sexual with him, or was there more? Did he feel engaged in the same way she did? Only time would sort that out, Keira told herself.

She left the bathroom and found that Nick had not yet returned to the bedroom. She laid her clothes on a cane armchair. She liked the white and lemon and lime-green furnishings of the room. Bright and beachy, she thought. The floor was of polished wood, although there were several mats for softness underfoot.

Her gaze kept shying away from the bed.

It had a bad effect on her nervous system.

Keira never liked to feel pressured. She instinctively resisted such a state of affairs. Her feet automatically took her across the room to the sliding glass doors. Stepping to the veranda railing gave her an immediate sense of relief or release. Being closed into a room, or a situation, was not a good idea, she decided. It encroached on free choice.

A light breeze wafted through her hair. The sound of the surf crashing onto the beach seemed very close. She lifted her gaze to the night sky, searching out the constellation of the Southern Cross, another sign that she was home.

"I give you the moon and the stars," came Nick's voice behind her.

She turned, laughing. He stood in the doorway, a mug of steaming coffee in each hand. Keira's laughter choked in her throat as she was assailed by the overwhelming impact of his strong masculinity, which the casual garb of a scarlet *yukata* seemed to emphasise . . . dramatically.

Apparently there was a second bathroom in the house because his hair was a mass of tight damp curls from showering. The loose cotton robe gaped almost to his waist, revealing the firm delineation of flesh and muscle and a sprinkle of black curls arrowing down from the base of his throat. Scarlet and black. The colours of the devil, Keira thought. But there was nothing satanic about Nick's face. The blue eyes promised heaven. His jaw was shiny from having been freshly shaven, and a tangy male scent drifted from his skin.

Keira had never felt heart-wrenching desire before. She had been mildly attracted to quite a few men, but she had never before experienced the heart-pounding, mind-blasting desire to know a man's body with absolute intimacy, to feel it, taste it, merge with it to the exclusion of all other considerations.

She felt it now with mesmerising force. She was struck speechless, motionless, caught in a thrall of intense fascination, staring at him.

He stepped onto the veranda, moved to her side, placed the mugs on the wide railing. As though he emitted a magnetic force she turned towards him, drinking in his profile, which seemed carved out of stone in the moonlight. Until he threw his dazzling white smile at her.

"Is this what you wanted, Delilah?" he asked softly.

"It must be," she whispered, then wrenched her gaze from his face and lifted it to the stars again. She wanted more, of course. Much more. But if the fates were kind, that would come. This intense physical response to him, this compelling recognition that no-one else had ever evoked, was the beginning. For anything to develop there had to be a beginning. From there it would expand like the universe, for good or ill. She saw a falling star and wished on it. Let it be good....

"What did you mean by king tide?"

Her heart jolted at this voicing of her private thought. Her gaze dropped sharply to the probing inquiry in his. "I said those words?"

He nodded. "Just as you were falling asleep in the car."

She frowned. She wished she hadn't said them. They were too revealing. The thought of explaining the concept behind them made Keira feel even more vulnerable. If Nick was not in sympathy...

Better to shrug it off. "Time and tide waits for no man," she said glibly.

"And?" he prompted.

"And what?"

"And I think there's much more to it."

He was too perceptive. She picked up her mug and began sipping the coffee. Her skin was prickling with sensitivity from her very nearness to him. If she let things proceed as Nick clearly meant them to—if she rode this king tide she felt building inside her—would he love her? Could he be as good as he said he was? Would it lead to the ultimate fulfilment she craved?

He was waiting for an answer. Keira suddenly realised that the best way of finding out how closely they could come together was to reveal her innermost thoughts. There was no point in holding back. If Nick's response revealed they were not mentally attuned it was better to know now, before she plunged in too far.

"Things happen. Sometimes suddenly. Unexpectedly," she mused softly. "Circumstances create an opportunity that is written in sand. Often it's not recognised until it's too late. The chance is gone. It evaporates. Or you misread the situation. And it's still gone. You must have experienced it yourself, the sense of time and place, of opportunity never to be repeated."

"Yes," he agreed quietly. "I've found that in my life, too."

Keira smiled, deeply pleased that he had understood. She turned her gaze out to sea, remembering the lines she had learnt so long ago. "The idea comes from a speech in Shakespeare. Nothing to do with nature, Nick."

"Tell me the idea," he urged.

She flicked him a teasing look. "You really want me to quote Shakespeare?"

He smiled. "An adman takes quotes from any source that can spread the message most effectively."

She eyed him uncertainly. "You might misinterpret it."

"Then you can correct me."

Because she wanted to share with him, to understand him and be understood, Keira decided to chance it. Her gaze automatically returned to the ocean as she spoke the words that had influenced so many of the choices she had made in her life.

"There is a tide in the affairs of men,
Which, taken at the flood, leads on to fortune;
Omitted, all the voyage of their life
Is bound in shallows and in miseries.
On such a full sea are we now afloat,
And we must take the current when it serves,
Or lose our ventures."

There was a long silence before Nick spoke. "You think coming with me will lead on to fortune?" he asked in a flat, toneless voice.

Disappointment stabbed her heart. His thinking was cynically twisted by the power and position his wealth had given him. "I don't think Shakespeare was using the word fortune in the way you're using it, Nick," she said with dry irony. "There is more to fortune than gold. There's happiness, well-being..."

"Besides which, you can't be bought," Nick cut in with an apologetic grimace. "Sorry...wrong note. I stand corrected once again. And I beg your pardon for the lapse into shallow judgement. I should be learning faster."

Keira shrugged. "This isn't a matter of learning. You either feel it or you don't. Besides, a neap tide can either lift up or destroy. I don't know what's going to happen. I don't know which you will do to me, Nick. That's up to you."

She gave him a crooked smile. "But if I hadn't come with you, I'd never have known. I guess I had to find out. I wasn't going to spend the rest of my life wondering what I might have missed."

He cupped her face, keeping it tilted to his as he searched her eyes long and hard. "I don't know what to think of you," he said at last. "But I'm glad you're here."

He took the coffee mug from her and set it on the railing. Then he gently took her by the shoulders and turned her to face him. Was it going to happen now? Did she want it to? Keira's pulse leapt into overdrive as her heart began to pound erratically. Her breathing became fast and shallow. She had never been involved in anything like this before.

But he didn't draw her into an embrace. There was a smile in his eyes, a soft curve of sensual whimsy on his lips. He dropped his hands from her shoulders, and from the pouched looseness of the *yukata* above his belted waist, he withdrew a sprig of frangipani flowers.

"They make leis of these in the Pacific Islands," he said, presenting the fragrant cluster to her. "They're flowers of greeting, for happiness and well-being and for celebrating momentous occasions...and for lingering, loving memories. They're the flowers of love."

Either he was a very fast learner indeed, tapping into the needs pulsing through her, or he was expressing what he thought and felt. Keira desperately hoped it was the latter. It had to be. Or she would never have the confidence to follow her instincts again.

He plucked one of the perfect blooms and positioned it over her left ear, winding a long silky tress of her hair around it to fasten it there. He took another bloom, positioning it higher, then another and another, outlining her face with flowers in such a slow,

deliberate way that it seemed like a reverent cere-
mony, as though he were dressing her as his bride.

The heavy fragrance surrounded her, so sweetly intoxicating that Keira felt she was floating on a full
sea, buoyed by currents of exhilarating happiness and
glorious well-being. She watched Nick's dark handsome face, so intent on what he was doing, so bril-
liantly lit with satisfaction when he completed the halo
effect with a flower over her right ear and his eyes
roved over his handiwork.

"And so it is," he murmured, half-wonderingly.

And so it is. Keira's heart pounded. Because it had
to be!

Then he smiled at her as he took the stripped frangipani sprig from her hands, plucked the last bloom
from it and tossed the empty stalk away. "I want you
to remember the scent of this flower all your life," he
murmured, brushing the soft petals over her lips, under her nose, around her face, gently closing her eyelids, as though he was anointing her skin with the
velvet perfume.

His voice whispered its caress into her mind, tones
deeper than normal. "Remember how I loved you this
night, with the moon and stars overhead and the roll
of the sea beating its eternal rhythm."

She opened her eyes, not seeing the moon and the
stars, only him. Not hearing the sea, only the thunderous drum of her heart and the sweet echo of his
words of love, inextricably mixed with the sweet,
heady smell of the frangipani.

He curved his hand around her cheek, tilted her chin
up, bent and kissed her lips, lightly, softly, meaning-

fully. Not fierce demanding passion—Keira knew that would come later—but a touching, a tasting, a reaching out . . . a beginning.

The tug on her soul grew stronger, irresistible. She tasted him, needing to know more of this man who could simultaneously project unlimited passion and exquisite restraint. She felt her lips swell with sensitivity against his, heightening the contact, the movement, the awareness, the sensation of being one with him.

His mouth moved away from hers, grazing up her cheeks, over her eyes, her temples, her forehead. She wanted to press into the warmth she felt emanating from his body, to touch him, yet the desire to reach out was entangled with the fascination of savouring what he was doing to her.

His hand slid under her hair to the nape of her neck and tilted her head back. His eyes locked onto hers, dark and turbulent, seeking answers from her. "Is this how sirens enslave men's souls, simply by being?"

"It's you enchanting me, Nick," she replied huskily. "Is it possible. . ." Her mouth dried up. It was so important, so critical.

"Anything is possible," he assured her, a deep indomitable throb of conviction in his voice.

She swallowed hard and cast caution to the winds. "Is it possible to fall in love at first sight, Nick?" she asked.

His expression softened as his gaze roved around her face. "I think it must be," he whispered.

He trailed his hand down her throat, feathering her skin with the lightest fingertip touch, grazing slowly down the deep valley between her breasts, narrowly parting the loose edges of her robe to her waist. Keira held her breath—whether in fear or anticipation she didn't know—but he made no attempt to undress her.

He took her hands, which were still clasped in front of her, and spread their palms over the bare heated flesh below his throat. She felt his chest rise and fall as his breathing quickened. He began stroking her arms, her shoulders, her back, drawing her closer and closer to him. She could see the pulse at the base of his throat beating fast, beating for her, and any doubts Keira might have had about Nick's feelings for her were drowned in a wave of blessed certainty.

This wasn't lust. It was loving. Beautiful, caring loving. Keira moved her hands, sliding them under the loose covering and over his strongly muscled shoulders. Her man, she thought fiercely, and knew she had reached the point of no return. Until now she could have stopped. That was no longer possible.

As though Nick sensed her surrender to him, he enfolded her in his arms, heating her flesh with his, crushing her against him. His mouth sought hers, and the urgency that had been missing before burst into wild hungry kisses. Keira thrust her hands into the thick black curls above the nape of his neck, revelling in the tempestuous rush of his need for her.

It was right. Yes, it was right, she thought exultantly. Her senses seemed to have taken on a supernormal quality. His hard muscular body was imprinting itself on hers and it felt so good, as though she had been formed precisely for this, to yield her softness to his moulding. The taste of him was as heady as the perfume that clung around them. She moved her face so that Nick could kiss her throat, her neck, behind her ear, laying warm sensual trails with his tongue as she undulated in his arms, wantonly making herself available and vulnerable as he found one fresh target after another for his sultry, warming, intoxicating kisses.

He found her mouth again and stayed there for a long time, passion giving way to a slow deliberate sensuality, to a mesmerising contact where their lips were barely touching, yet her awareness of him had been fanned to such a fever pitch that it was like an exquisite, almost ethereal floating, a hazy cloud of harmony and pleasure.

He drew open her *yukata* to reveal her breasts to the heavy atmosphere of the night, to the moon and the stars and the scented breeze from the sea. Then he pressed them to his own hard heated flesh, claiming them as his possession, denying them to the rest of the world. Keira hugged him so tightly that his hands were free to find erotic spots on her back, her long-limbed thighs. She trembled under his every touch, wanting more, her whole body alive with anticipation for all that could happen between them.

He pushed the sleeves of her *yukata* from her arms, shrugged out of his, and both garments fell at their feet. Then they were together again, totally abandoned in their nakedness, claiming each other like pagan entities in the moonlight, their bodies exulting in the sharper, more compelling intimacy, slithering, sliding, dancing to a mounting inner rhythm that could not be denied.

Keira knew that meaningless incoherent sounds were breaking from her lips as Nick kissed her almost senseless. Her thighs trembled against the power of his. The aggressive maleness of his body excited her beyond anything she had ever known, igniting some mysterious chain-reaction of responses in her that seemed to melt her bones.

The thought ran through her mind that she would never be the same again. And she didn't care. She knew only Nick, felt only for him, lived only for him. If she was his pleasure, then he could have all of her, for always and forever.

He swept her with him onto a wide lounge, and there seemed to be flowers all around her. Nick scooped them up over her breasts, caressing her with them, following their perfumed trails with his lips. She writhed in ecstatic pleasure at the sheer eroticism of his lovemaking. She felt, time after time, that there could be no more exquisite pleasure than this, but then he would excite a new crescendo of sensation, and all Keira could do was cling to him in helpless surrender to his control.

The greatest satisfaction came when at last he entered her, and the full heavy surge of him inside her was the ultimate answer to all the feelings he had evoked. Keira moved slowly, rhythmically, undulating under his fierce insistent pressure, her pleasure being heightened in continuous waves. She was not just melting around him. Her body was doing something that she had no idea it was capable of. It was as if her blood was thickening and every cell in her body was fusing into something else entirely, like a metamorphosis that radiated from Nick's possession of her.

We are becoming one, she thought, then all thought disintegrated with everything else, and Keira found a languid peace that went beyond peace. She was in her own private valley, a world of contentment and sunshine where nothing ever went wrong.

But Nick had held himself back for her sake, and the desire for absolute completion urged her to help him fulfil his desire. She wanted him to savour the full joy of what had happened between them, and she encouraged him to surge into her to his fullest limits, stroking him, kissing him, mumbling meaningless words until with a harsh animal cry he attained the blissful release that let him join her in the valley of peace.

He held her close to him for a long time after, his breathing slowly returning to normal. The heavy musky scent of their lovemaking mingled with the heady perfume of crushed frangipani blooms, permeating the night, creating a memory that would live on for the rest of Keira's life.

She felt so languorously content that she could have stayed where she was forever, idly looking at the stars, listening to the sea shifting the sands. So it was written, and so it has come to pass, she thought, savouring the warm, loving reality of holding the man of her dreams in her arms. She could not have imagined anything more wonderful, more perfect.

When Nick levered himself up to look at her, she smiled, her eyes luminous with happiness, her face glowing with the knowledge of a new life, a new dimension of living. He kissed her softly, lingeringly.

"I think your name should have been Lorelei, not Delilah," he murmured, smoothing strands of hair away from her face.

She wanted to tell him her name was Keira, but now was not the right time. This was too perfect. She recoiled from the thought of explaining about Justin being her cousin, and the problem with Louise. Any talk about anyone else would be far too intrusive on the intimate mood of this moment. She would do it first thing in the morning.

A look of something like pain crossed Nick's face. He rolled onto his back, carrying her with him so that she lay with her head tucked under his chin, her cheek pressed over his heart. He held her there tightly for several long moments, then slowly relaxed his embrace and began to stroke her hair.

"What will I do with you?" he mused softly, as though she were a conundrum he couldn't figure out.

"Love me," she answered with a sweet sigh of contentment. "Love me always."

His chest rose and fell in a much deeper sigh. "Perhaps I will," he murmured. "Perhaps all the rest is irrelevant. And it is only you that matters."

Keira smiled to herself. It was what she wanted to hear. And tonight's experience was only a beginning. The future shone very brightly in her mind's eye, much brighter than the moon and the stars, and full of glorious warm sunshine. The promise that he had held out to her had been fulfilled. It could only go on. And get better.

She fell asleep under the slow enchantment of his entrancing, caressing hands. She was vaguely conscious of being carried and set down against soft pillows. Her body moved instinctively to snuggle against the lovely warmth of his, and her forehead puckered in protest as a wrong name whispered into her ear.

"Delilah."

Keira . . . it should be Keira.

But the long journey to this moment took its toll, dragging her into a deep, fathomless sleep that knew nothing of the man beside her, the man who was savagely wishing she wasn't what she appeared to be.

CHAPTER SIX

NICK WAS GONE from her side when Keira woke in the morning. She felt bereft until she saw the note propped on the bedside table. The sense of relief when she read it was deep and intense.

"Gone for provisions. Back soon."

She wished he had signed it, "Love, Nick," but it didn't matter. His actions and words last night were enough to hug to her heart. Heaven, she thought, and stretched luxuriously in the king-size bed. Nick's bed. Which she would share with him from now on. Forever and ever.

A crumpled flower caught her eye. She picked it up and brushed the soft petals around her face, remembering, exulting in the memory. She breathed in the heady scent and felt her body clenching with other memories. Nick had been right. He had given her more love in an hour than any other man could give her in a lifetime. Keira had no doubt about that.

Morning sunshine was streaming in through the glass doors. It was going to be a beautiful day, Keira thought. The best day of her life. She rolled off the bed and headed for the bathroom, eager to be ready for Nick's return.

There were still flowers tangled in her hair, their petals browning at the edges now. She carefully removed them. She had a sudden fancy to cast them into the sea and let them float on the current. She did not want these special flowers thrown into a rubbish bin. To her, they were like a bridal bouquet.

Having showered and freshened up as best she could, making use of a new toothbrush from a supply that Nick obviously kept for guests, and a comb that looked equally unused, Keira wandered into the bedroom and took the liberty of looking into the wall cupboards for something to wear. She wanted to go down to the beach. Her little black dress wasn't suitable for that, and she wanted something shorter than the *yukata*. She didn't think Nick would mind if she raided his wardrobe this once.

A row of T-shirts caught her eye. She chose a green one. It made a sloppy mini dress with her gold chain belt cinching it in around her waist. She also borrowed a pair of stretch underpants. There was something terribly intimate about wearing Nick's underpants. And deliciously sexy.

Keira laughed at herself. She didn't normally have this kind of awareness, but this morning was different. Her whole life was different. The focus of it had changed dramatically. Everything circled around Nick Sarazin.

She found a straw hat, scooped the wilting flowers into its crown and was at the glass doors leading onto the veranda when it occurred to her that she should leave Nick a note in case he returned before she did.

She quickly retraced her steps to the bedside table and added her own message to his.

"Gone down to the beach. Back soon."

The double sun lounger on the veranda bore no trace of last night's lovemaking. Nick must have swept everything clear while she slept this morning, Keira thought, and felt vaguely disappointed. She would have gathered those flowers, too, if they'd still been there.

A flight of steps at one end of the veranda led down to a lawn that spread to the sand. It was barely twenty metres across the beach to the water. The surf was relatively gentle this morning, no huge crashing waves. Keira waded in, enjoying the swirl of the water around her ankles and calves.

She had finished casting the frangipani blooms on a receding wave when she saw a larger one beginning to swell. A big dumper, she thought, and realising it might swamp her makeshift dress, she turned quickly and ran for the safety of the beach, laughing with sheer joy in the morning, the sunshine, the water and sand.

Then she caught sight of Nick, watching her from the veranda, and waved at him in happy greeting. He looked so athletic and devastatingly handsome in white shorts and T-shirt.

"Stay there! I'll join you!" he called out, returning her wave.

He turned into the bedroom before Keira found breath enough to answer. She didn't particularly want to stay where she was. She had done what she had come out to do—the flowers were all adrift—and her stomach felt very empty. Breakfast seemed like a much better idea.

She ran up to the house, thinking of cooking a stack of bacon and eggs if Nick had thought to buy them. She expected him to be in the bedroom, changing into swim gear, but he wasn't. Then she heard his voice talking to someone and followed the sound down a hallway to a well-equipped kitchen. Nick had his back turned to her, a telephone receiver nursed against his ear as he spoke in sharp, clipped tones.

"I assure you, it's fixed. You have nothing more to worry about on that score."

A business call, Keira thought, and waited quietly and patiently so as not to interrupt his train of thought. Taking off with her, as he had last night, was undoubtedly causing a few problems. However, that idea was totally shattered when Nick next spoke, his tone one of mounting exasperation.

"Louise, I promise you she won't be having anything more to do with Justin."

Keira froze, the words and implications too frightful to relate to herself. Yet it had to be. Nick listened for a moment, but his next words put the issue beyond doubt.

"It was *my* bed she shared last night. Not his. And I expect to keep her with me. In fact, I made damned sure she'll have no inclination whatsoever to stray from my side. I don't lose a woman until I want to, Louise. So stop being hysterical. And just for once, do something constructive about patching up your marriage. Have the baby, for God's sake! I've done what you asked me to do. Now you do what you have to do, because I'm finished with your schemes."

Keira clutched at the door jamb as she felt the blood draining from her face. Her mind whirled in sickening circles. Justin asking her to seduce a man away from Louise... Louise asking Nick to get "the brazen hussy" away from her husband, to eliminate any possibility of her returning.

Nothing to do with love.

Cold-blooded, calculated seduction.

Nick Sarazin had never thought—not for one moment—that she was the one for him. There had been no sincerity in anything he had said and done. All a performance, a beautifully contrived performance, an evil, satanic performance!

Keira shuddered in revulsion. Never had she felt so despoiled, so ravaged, so cheated and betrayed. Even her own cousin had let her down, knowing she was going with Louise's *man*.

Nick Sarazin, the Australian playboy, notching up a Delilah on his belt of conquests.

Her stomach churned. Bile rose in her throat, and perhaps she made some stricken sound choking it down. Nick suddenly spun around and saw her. They stared at each other, the horror of realising what she had overheard stamped on his face, the horror of having been his victim stamped on hers.

Keira knew then what Louise had felt last night. She wanted to claw out his deceiving blue eyes and disfigure his darkly beautiful face. She wanted to maim and kill and destroy until there was nothing left of him to remind her of the man she thought he had been. The violent passion that flooded through her was such a frightening, alien thing that it spurred her into flight.

She ran blindly. Anywhere away from him, anywhere. She stumbled down the hallway, through the bedroom, onto the veranda, down the steps. And behind her he called that hated name. "Delilah! Delilah!" Hoarse and urgent and demanding that she stop.

Demanding. So much he had demanded of her, and taken and used, abusing her feelings for him with such callous disregard. A devil, uncaring what hell he sent her to, uncaring as long as *he* got *his* way!

She staggered through the sand towards the water. The tide was going out. Her flowers were gone. Gone like her love. And there was black despair in the heart she had opened to him, desolation in the soul she had opened to him, betrayal in the mind she had opened to him.

"Delilah." He was coming after her.

"No!" she screamed, shaking her head in anguished denial. "Keira! Keira!"

He didn't stop.

She couldn't bear him near her. She plunged into the water, welcoming the cold buffeting of the waves. A glance over her shoulder showed Nick ploughing in after her. Damn him to hell forever! she thought savagely. Didn't he know it was time to stop? Couldn't he see that nothing could be gained by pursuing her now?

Then a wall of water crashed on top of her. Caught off guard by the dumper, Keira was swept off her feet and tumbled into a maelstrom of sea and sand. Hard biting hands gripped under her arms and hauled her out of the churning turbulence. She was coughing and spluttering too much to put up any fight. Then she was dumped again, on warm dry sand this time, and her hated rescuer sat himself beside her, breathing hard.

Keira did some hard breathing herself once she had retched up all the sea water she had swallowed. Control was what she needed—iron-clad control. Nick Sarazin could talk himself blue in the face but she wouldn't let him get to her. Never again!

"Are you okay?" he rasped.

"Yes," she bit out. "Go away."

"Not until I explain."

"There's nothing to explain," she sliced at him, then turned her head away in contemptuous dismissal.

He was not deterred. "Louise works for me."

Keira didn't want to hear a whole stack of self-serving lies. "I hope she's good at her job!" she sniped.

"And she had a problem—"

"Which is very certainly your problem now!"

"—with her husband. I was trying to sort it out."

"You have succeeded admirably."

"Won't you please listen?" he demanded in exasperation.

"No!"

"Why not?"

"Because I know perfectly well what you've done. You seduced me."

"I did not!"

"Yes, you did!"

"Only a little bit. The rest of it was—"

"Too despicable to contemplate!" she blazed at him, her green eyes stripping him of any defence through the dangling rats' tails of her hair.

"It was beautiful!" he protested angrily. "You were beautiful! The whole thing was beautiful!"

Beautiful lies, she thought savagely. Even to saying "always," deliberately lying so she would have "no inclination to stray from his side." He probably made every woman he wanted to seduce believe that he was the one for her. *Made for each other!* Keira would never forgive him for that. The passionate hatred welled up again.

"Yes, well," she drawled. "I expect an adman knows all about setting a stage and creating an effect." She raised her hand in savage mockery. "I salute you! You're the grand master of the game! I now appreciate why you've been so very, very successful."

He looked darkly furious, the blue eyes glittering daggers at her. "You tell me, what point is there in destroying what we've got together? It's plain stupid, Delilah!"

Keira rose to her feet. Her legs felt shaky and she knew she looked a total mess, but she disdainfully ignored the sagging wet T-shirt now coated with gritty sand. She raked back the long strands of hair that clung to her face and neck like lank seaweed, tilted her chin high, looked at him in towering scorn and delivered her judgement. "We've got nothing!"

"The hell we haven't!"

"And you can stop calling me Delilah! My name is Keira!" she flung at him. Having delivered the ultimate exit line, she turned and started marching along the beach, seething at the crass arrogance that expected her to overlook his rotten manoeuvring.

"Where do you think you're going?"

He had jumped to his feet and fallen into step beside her. The demand in his voice was typical. Keira's resentment of his attitude reached new heights.

"Away," she snapped.

"Where?"

"The last person I'd tell that to is you."

"Will you stop being so damned unreasonable?" he yelled at her. Then he dragged in a deep breath and lowered his tone to one of soothing persuasion. "This is ridiculous. Let's go back to the house. We'll have a shower together. I'll wash all the sand off your body, dry you off with a big fluffy towel. Then we can relax on the bed and I'll tell you in detail just how reasonable I've been."

If the arch-seducer thought he could wheedle a repeat performance with her, he was a very slow learner. She favoured him with a look of acid contempt. "Pigs might fly!"

He glowered at her. "Why did you say your name is Keira?"

"None of your business."

"But it's not Delilah, is it?"

"No."

"You were out to seduce *me,* weren't you?" he accused.

"Now that *is* ridiculous!" she retorted in seething bitterness. "I'd never dream of being so hard-hearted, calculating, mean and despicable. Not like some other people I could mention."

His laugh was a derisive bark. "I bet you thought you were seducing me and that's why you're in such a huff. A little dent to the female pride."

She pulled up for a breather. It was heavy going through the sand. Besides, it gave her the opportunity to slap Nick Sarazin down, metaphorically speaking.

She looked him straight in the eye and said, "I think you're stupid."

"What?" His disbelief in such an idea was written all over his face.

"I think you're stupid," Keira repeated emphatically.

An angry flush tinged his cheekbones. The blue eyes blazed with a turbulent mix of emotions. Paramount seemed to be self-disgust. "You're damned well right! I am stupid! For falling in love with a woman like you!"

This clenched-teeth declaration gave Keira pause for thought. But only for a moment. It was another one of his lies to keep her with him. "I'm leaving," she stated determinedly.

"Because I'm falling in love with you?" he demanded incredulously.

"Because I don't trust you one iota!"

"Ha!" he scoffed. "You've got the roles reversed. I don't trust you. Remember?"

"Too bad!" Having caught her breath, she set off again, determinedly ploughing on, away from him.

"What's your relationship with Justin Brooks?" He was beside her again, stubbornly persisting in being demanding.

"Since you're on such good terms with Louise, get her to ask him," she advised sarcastically.

"You're impossible!"

No, just badly hurt, Keira thought. And he was frustrated because he wasn't getting the pleasure he had anticipated out of his successful seduction. He was losing a woman before he chose to. And, of course, she might go back to Justin and that would mean Nick Sarazin losing face to Louise. A *huge* dent to *his* pride!

"You can't go anywhere looking like that!" he argued, obviously deciding an appeal to common sense might work.

"Yes, I can," Keira retorted, not giving an inch.

"You don't have any money," he said triumphantly.

"Then I'll have to get by without it."

"You are *bloody* impossible!" he yelled, reduced to swearing by her intransigence.

"Yes," she agreed calmly. "To you I always will be."

Something like an animal growl issued from his throat. "We'll see about that," he muttered fiercely.

He moved so fast Keira could not take any evasive action. He turned on her, tackling her like a rugby forward and hoisting her over his shoulder.

Keira kicked and beat at him in total disregard of her firm belief in non-violence. Nick Sarazin totally ignored any damage she might do to him. Holding her in a relentless grip, he strode manfully up the beach to the house, determined on having his way with her.

"I hate you!" she screamed.

"Hate is the reverse side of love," he replied with infuriating smugness.

"I'm not staying with you." She wished she could kick *him* in the place it hurt most.

"That's okay. We'll work it the other way. I'll stay with you."

"No, you won't!"

"You're not going back to Justin Brooks. He's a married man."

"Put me down, you rotten bully!" Keira cried bitterly, finding some outlet for her rage in thumping Nick Sarazin's buttocks as hard as she could.

"Would you like to claw my back? I find that exciting, too."

"Oh!" She tried twisting so she could cuff his head, but couldn't quite make it. "I'll get you for this!" she cried in frustration.

"That sounds even more exciting."

"You're enjoying this, aren't you? Playing a big bully caveman," she raged.

"It has its moments."

"It won't get you anywhere. I can promise you that."

"On the contrary. It's got us both back to the house." He started up the veranda steps. "In another minute or two we'll be in the shower together. And then I'm going to kiss you senseless, since I can't talk common sense to you."

"You just try it, Nick Sarazin!" Keira threatened, premeditated murder in her heart. "I'll bite your lips. I'll bite your tongue. I'll claw your skin off. You'll be bleeding like a stuck pig by the time I'm through with you. And don't count out other more painful damage, either," she added as he crossed the bedroom floor and she caught sight of the bed she had shared with him.

"On second thought," he said, pushing open the bathroom door, "I think I'll simply leave you here to cool off for a while."

"A very wise decision," she said sarcastically.

He turned on the taps in the shower, tipped her into it, sidestepped her swinging fist and went off laughing, shutting the door with a triumphant bang after him.

Keira fumed with mountainous outrage. If Nick Sarazin thought he'd won anything with his brute tactics, he had a big surprise coming. She would show him he couldn't tell her what she could or could not do. She could do any darned thing she set her mind to!

She left the taps running, marched out of the bathroom, through the bedroom, along the veranda, down the steps, around the side of the house, reached the street and set off for the far, far distance, for the great stream of humanity, for a world without Nick Sarazin!

Brutally unshackled from the ties of a false love, she was a free spirit again. Above everything else, Keira Mary Brooks was a survivor, and she would survive Nick Sarazin, too!

Given enough time to put the soul-destroying experience behind her.

CHAPTER SEVEN

A BLACK JAGUAR SPORTS sedan pulled up at the side of the road ahead of her. Keira had no idea how far she had walked, or in what direction she was going, or how much time had passed since she had left the beach house, but she had no doubt about the owner of the car even before Nick Sarazin stepped out of it.

He was clean and spruce in stone-washed black jeans and a white sports shirt. Expensive Reeboks on his feet. Even his casual clothes reeked of money and class, confirming his playboy status, Keira thought savagely. He rounded the car, opened the passenger door and stood waiting beside it with his arrogant brand of self-assurance.

"This has gone far enough, Keira," he said sternly when she stopped dead and turned away from him, pointedly waiting for a car to pass before crossing to the other side of the road. "Get in the car and I'll take you wherever you want to go."

"I don't get into cars with strangers," she sniped at him.

"I'm not a stranger," he grated.

"Yes, you are. Your mind is totally alien to mine," she retorted fiercely.

"If you don't get into the car, I'll pick you up and put you there," he threatened.

Her green eyes blazed a promise of quick and sudden death. "Do you want your car smashed?"

He thumped the hood in exasperation. "For God's sake! Be reasonable. You can't go walking around like that. You might as well be naked."

"It's *my* skin," she hurled at him, then set off across the road, leaving him swearing and cursing.

However, his comment about being naked did sink home. In her distraught state of mind, Keira had forgotten how revealing a wet T-shirt was. When she reached the other side of the road, she tried picking the clinging fabric away from her breasts, but it only flapped and stuck to her skin again when she let it go. It would dry eventually, she told herself, but she felt extremely conscious of the problem as she trudged along.

The black Jaguar pulled up in front of her again. He must have made a U-turn, she thought, as Nick Sarazin leapt out of the driver's side and planted himself in her path. Keira looked across to the other side of the road, wondering how often she was going to have to zigzag before her erstwhile lover got the message that he was dead as far as she was concerned.

"All right!" he said, holding up his hands in an appeasing gesture. "I was wrong. And stupid. I'm not going to manhandle you again. I'm just concerned about you, Keira."

"I don't want you concerned about me. I can look after myself," she argued coldly. "I've been doing it for twenty-six years and I'm very good at it, thank you. If you'd just go away and get out of my life, I'll get on very well by myself.''

He didn't like that idea one bit. In fact he was beginning to look quite anxious and desperate. It gave Keira considerable satisfaction to see his self-assurance cracking. Time he learnt he couldn't have everything his way.

"How can you keep on doing this to yourself?" he demanded. His gaze dropped to the clearly delineated shape of her breasts. Looking at them seemed to increase his anguish. He wrenched his eyes up again. His hands sliced the air in agitation. "Without money or—"

"I've been in stickier situations and got out of them," Keira informed him scornfully, folding her arms to stop him from looking at her body.

He didn't like that thought, either. "Would you mind telling me how?"

"All I've got to do is keep walking until I find a policeman. Or a policeman finds me. One or the other always happens. The police are always kind and helpful in situations like this. Particularly when I tell them in detail what you did to me. Not only will they look after me, but they'll keep their eyes open for *you*. One false step..."

"Oh, great!" he muttered angrily. The blue eyes blazed fierce resentment at her. "And what do you propose to tell them? That you've escaped from a mad rapist?"

"What a good idea!" she agreed with acid sweetness. "How clever of you to think of such a thing.

However, I don't think I will use it. My aim, at this point in time, is to forget that you ever existed."

An angry red slashed across his cheekbones. The blue eyes glittered a fierce challenge at her. "That's not what you felt last night, Keira," he rasped.

Pain stabbed into her heart and welled into her eyes. She hastily looked away, blinking rapidly, mortified that his words had slipped past her guard. "If you had any feelings you wouldn't remind me of that," she muttered fiercely.

"I'm sorry." He sighed. Deeply. "I truly am sorry. I'm desperately sorry that you feel so hurt. I'll make amends. Please give me that chance, Keira."

She shook her head, far too disillusioned with him to take any more chances. "You're not the man I thought you were."

"You're not the woman I thought you were, either," he said softly. "Is Keira another alias, or is it truly your real name?"

She supposed that was fair comment but it didn't make any difference. "Only the person counts. Not their names." She turned weary washed-out eyes to his. "Last night you pressured me into a decision. Now or never. You've had the now, Nick. This is the never." Her mouth curled into a smile of bitter irony. "The tide wasn't a king tide after all. It ebbed very suddenly this morning."

He took a deep breath. His face sagged into grim lines. The blue eyes begged forbearance. "It sounded bad, Keira. That was all. What I said to Louise was for a purpose—"

"Everything you've said to me, Nick, was for a purpose. I understand it all," she said with quiet, but pointed emphasis. "You and I are *not* made for each other. We have different values. So please, do the decent thing for once."

"Which is?"

"Let me go."

He paused, reflected, considered. The blue eyes questioned the judgement in hers for a long time. Keira's gaze remained steadfast. There was not the slightest wavering in her resolution to put this encounter with Nick Sarazin behind her. Eventually he reached a decision.

"I can't let you go like this, Keira. Not this way," he said with disturbing intensity. "You're a walking invitation for trouble, with a capital *T.* And I do happen to be concerned enough to want to prevent it. Tell me where to take you, and I'll take you there. When I'm sure you're safe and well looked after, I'll let you go."

She considered the proposal. Nick looked sincere, sounded sincere, but she knew he couldn't be trusted. Nevertheless, she was footsore, tired and hungry, and the alternatives to trusting him were not exactly attractive.

"Would you take me to Justin?" she asked.

His grimace was followed by a sigh of grudging resignation. "Yes. Even to him. If that's what you want."

"He's got my things," she explained. "I'll have to ring him."

Nick gave her an ironic smile. "The car phone is at your disposal."

Still she hesitated. "Do you swear this is a genuine offer?" she asked suspiciously.

"Why would you doubt it?"

"You told me you break the rules."

"I never break my word." He moved to the passenger door and opened it for her.

Keira paused for a moment. "I'll make a mess of your car," she warned, all too aware of her wet, gritty state.

"Since I seem to have made a mess of everything else, that is the least of my concerns," he replied.

She was suddenly very weary of fighting. With a dull sense of fatalism she pushed her legs forward and entered the car, oddly uncaring that it was stupid to trust Nick Sarazin in any shape or form. Somehow it was no longer important. Nothing seemed to be important. She felt lost in a way she had never felt before, as though her sense of direction had been taken away.

Again he fastened her seat belt for her, because she didn't think of it. He didn't chide her for her negligence. He didn't say anything. He started the car and drove at a relatively sedate pace. Whether it was the events of the morning catching up with her, or whether it was because she was sitting still instead of walking, or simply from delayed shock, Keira didn't know, but she started shivering and couldn't stop.

Nick turned the air-conditioning to warm, but the rise in temperature made no difference. Even her teeth began chattering. When they reached East Gosford, Nick pulled the car into a shopping centre.

"Stay here. I'll get you a coffee and something hot to eat," he said in a kindly tone.

"Thank you," she whispered gratefully.

"I'll be as quick as I can," he assured her.

She nodded, tears blurring her eyes at his consideration. She was a mess, physically, mentally and emotionally. Any kind of control seemed to have slipped out of her grasp. She concentrated hard on getting it back. She had to call Justin and stop him from sending her bags to where she wouldn't be any more.

She took several deep breaths, picked up the car phone and dialled his home number. He was probably at his office, she thought distractedly, and tried to remember the number for information, but it eluded her. She had been out of Australia for too long. Luck, however, was on her side. Justin had not gone to work. He answered her call, much to Keira's relief.

"Justin, you haven't sent off my bags already, have you?" she asked shakily.

"Keira? Is that you?" He sounded unsure.

"Yes."

"It doesn't sound like you," he said, a frown in his voice.

"It's me. What have you done about my bags?"

"Everything's set," he assured her. "I've put five hundred dollars in cash in an envelope in your handbag, plus a cheque for the balance. The courier should be arriving here to pick them up any minute now."

"Cancel the courier, Justin. I don't want them sent. I'm on my way back to you."

"Here? You can't come here, Keira," he said anxiously. "Louise has agreed to have dinner with me tonight and I..."

"Justin, please." Her voice broke as tears rushed into her eyes. "I've got nowhere else to go," she sobbed.

"Keira?" He sounded incredulous. "What's happened? Why are you crying?"

"You should have told me, Justin," she burst out in bitter grievance, "that he was Louise's man. I did my best to help you. You should never have let me go with him, knowing who he was. You had to know."

"Keira, you liked him. You wanted to go with him," he justified himself vehemently.

"He only carried me off to get me away from you, Justin. Louise asked him to and he..." She couldn't go on. She broke down and wept uncontrollably. "I need you," she sobbed. "I need your help, Justin. Please..."

"What the hell did he do to you?" he burst out angrily.

"Enough," she choked out.

"I've never known you to cry about anything before!"

"Justin..." She gulped hard, trying to recover some control of her voice. "Can you book me into a hotel? Get my bags there for me? I'll stay out of your way. If you could do that for me."

"Come home to me, Keira. We'll have to try and sort things out with Louise! If she put that guy onto you—"

"No! No, I don't want to make trouble. A hotel. Please, Justin. No trouble. I don't want to be involved any more."

"Keira . . ." Troubled uncertainty.

"Please don't argue. I couldn't bear it."

"I'll kill the bastard!" he muttered fiercely, then forced himself into more productive thought. "A hotel. I'll get the best for you, Keira. A suite at the Regent. I'll send your bags over there right now. They'll be there waiting for you. All you'll have to do is give your name at the desk. Now what about getting there? Where are you?"

"Gosford."

"Do you want me to come and—"

"No. I can get to the Regent. Thank you."

"Family is family," he said strongly. "Don't worry, Keira. I'll look after you."

His support broke the dam again and Keira burst into another flood of tears. "Thank you," she choked out and fumbled the phone down. She never cried. Justin was right about that. She had always prided herself on being able to rise above such a show of weakness. Yet for some stupid reason she couldn't seem to stop crying. It was as if she had no say in it at all. Her body wasn't obeying any edicts from her mind.

She was even more of a shuddering wet mess when Nick Sarazin opened the passenger door. He muttered something savage under his breath, leaned across her, undid her safety belt, lifted her out of the car, set her on her feet, wrapped a soft mohair rug around her, then hugged her in a tight embrace.

"Did Justin Brooks let you down?" he asked gruffly.

"No." She snuffled.

He heaved a deep sigh. "Keira, I saw you talking on the phone."

"He's booking me into the Regent. Will you...will you take me there?"

"Yes. I'll take you there. If that's what you want," he added in a flat, unenthusiastic voice.

"It's what I want," she said.

"Then why are you crying, Keira?" Nick asked softly.

"Because..."

"Because why?" he prompted.

"Because I hate weak women."

"You're not weak, Keira." He tightened his embrace and his lips moved warmly over her temples.

Against all she knew to be true, Keira's heart kicked over, and she felt a terrible temptation to lean her head on his shoulder and surrender to whatever he wanted to do with her. Somehow she summoned up enough backbone to say, "You shouldn't be holding me like this." It came out very shakily.

"Why not?"

"Because—"

"I want to."

"—you don't mean it."

"Then why would I do it, Keira?" He rubbed her back in a gentle, comforting circular movement and kissed her some more, soft warm kisses that transmitted a soothing tenderness.

"I don't know," she quavered weakly. "You gave your word that you'd let me go."

"Yes. I did. But that doesn't mean I want to," he murmured huskily.

"You have to," she protested, beginning to feel painfully confused.

"If you say so," he agreed. His chest heaved and fell in another deep sigh. Then he helped her into the car and fastened her seat belt for her again. "The food should be ready by now. I'll be back in a minute," he said.

He closed the door and disappeared. Keira still shivered, but only in convulsive little bursts, not continuously. And it was a different kind of shivering, shot through with memories she had promised herself not to remember. Nick Sarazin wasn't the one. He shouldn't be able to affect her like this. Not now. She simply couldn't afford to be weak and stupid. It could only be destructive.

The mohair rug had a new smell about it. Nick must have gone and bought it, she reasoned, because he hadn't had it when he left the car. It was kind and thoughtful of him. Caring, too. But he couldn't really care. Maybe he felt guilty about what he'd done. He might have realised she wasn't a Delilah. She had certainly been mistaken about him, so she probably shouldn't judge him too harshly for being mistaken about her.

The whole situation was a mess.

She hoped Justin and Louise would get back together again.

At least one good thing should come out of it.

The door on the driver's side opened. Nick leaned down and held out two take-away cups of coffee. A plastic bag hung from his wrist, and the smell of hot fish and chips wafted from it. "Mind holding the coffee while I get in?" he asked.

She took the cups and he settled into the driver's seat and closed his door. Then he produced three cartons from the plastic bag, placed them on the console and opened them before retrieving his mug of coffee from her grasp.

"Prawn cutlets, fish pieces and chips. Help yourself," he invited with a warm smile that did nothing to settle Keira's equilibrium.

"Thank you," she murmured.

They ate in silence. The food was hot and freshly cooked and tasted very good to Keira. When they had finished, Nick produced paper napkins from the plastic bag to wipe their hands, then stacked the empty cartons and cups into it and slung it on the back seat.

"Feeling better now?"

She nodded. "Much better, thanks."

Again he smiled, doing another lot of damage to Keira's peace of mind and heart. It was because he was handsome and attractive, she told herself. Nothing more than that. Any man with those looks would make a woman's heart flutter a bit. His mind, however, was certainly not in tune with hers, and that was what counted.

He started the car and they got on their way again. "Have you known Justin Brooks long, Keira?" he asked, his tone one of idle curiosity.

"Yes," she answered briefly.

"How long?"

There seemed no point in not telling him the truth. "All my life. Our families were very close."

"Not any more?"

"My parents have been dead for quite some time."

"Do you have any brothers or sisters?"

"No."

"That must be rather lonely for you," he remarked in a sympathetic tone.

"I guess you don't miss what you've never had."

The bitter sense of betrayal came sweeping back. He had given her the sense of being loved with a performance that probably no other man she ever met would match. She wished now that she'd never had it. He had left her with a false measure to judge others by, deliberately going out of his way to implant it in her memory. Ego on his part, no doubt. Perhaps he was intent on building a reputation as a legendary lover. A born and bred adman, promoting himself as an artist of the bedroom.

"Do you have any family?" she asked, wondering what had made him the kind of man he was.

"I'm the youngest of four sons. And my parents are still alive," he answered easily.

"Do they approve of the way you live?"

He sliced her a hard, questioning look. "Do you seek approval from anyone for the way you live, Keira?"

"No," she had to admit. Although she privately added that she didn't make a specialty of seducing people, despite Justin's wild ideas about her.

"I guess they consider me the black sheep of the family," Nick confessed wryly. "My brothers are all in staid respectable professions. Law, medicine and architecture. They responded properly to my parents' expectations of their sons. I, being the youngest by several years, was allowed a little more leeway."

"You mean you were spoilt," Keira commented dryly.

He grinned at her, totally disrupting the regularity of her pulse. "Maybe they grew tired of setting goals for their children. Anyway, I was always inclined to go my own way. From time to time, they lined me up and chastened me with dire predictions about my future, but I guess, in a way, I was a free spirit, too. I wanted to try my wings. Which I did, to the tune of more dire predictions."

"But you eventually proved them wrong."

"Mmm, in some ways," he said consideringly. "I've ended up making more money than my brothers, but perhaps they've achieved more in a personal sense than I have."

"What do you mean?" Keira asked, curious to know what he found lacking in his life.

He shrugged. "They're all happily married with families."

"You envy that?" She couldn't keep the disbelief out of her voice. With his looks and wealth he could have had his choice of any number of marriageable women.

"Sometimes." He gave her a twisted little smile. "Sometimes they say they envy me my freewheeling life-style, but I suspect if they had it, they wouldn't feel comfortable with it."

"But you do." Of course he did. An accomplished seducer would never feel content with possessing only one woman.

"Do you, Keira?"

She frowned, not quite comprehending his question.

"I mean are you comfortable with your life?" he elaborated. "Do you feel you're missing out on something?"

The pain came back again. "Yes," she answered dully.

"What?"

What you offered me last night and took away this morning, she thought, and a wave of wretched misery swept away any further interest in the conversation. "Someone I could share my life with. Someone to love me," she answered flatly, then turned her head to the side window. "If you don't mind, Nick, I don't want to talk any more."

The tears welled again, but she was able to fight them this time. She stared unseeingly at the passing scenery, and after a while her eyelids grew heavy. She closed them and slipped easily into sleep. When she woke, feeling hot and flushed and unpleasantly sticky—the air in the car was very warm—they were already in Sydney, but she didn't recognise precisely what suburb they were travelling through, and they were not on a main thoroughfare.

"Why aren't we on the highway?" she asked.

"Less traffic this route," Nick answered.

Keira grimaced. Typical male. Women invariably stuck to a highway to get anywhere. It was the simplest, most straightforward route. Men always seemed compelled to find short cuts that proved them smarter than everyone else. Or perhaps it was some innate desire to beat the system and come out a winner.

In any event, the parting of the ways was fairly imminent, and the thought of never seeing Nick Sarazin again, never being with him again, suddenly brought a leaden weight to her heart. Simply the loss of a dream, Keira told herself. It had been such a beautiful dream last night. But she mustn't think about that. Maybe, some time in the future, she would be able to think about it without it hurting too much, but not now.

The car slowed. Keira frowned, not understanding the reason for it. There was no car slowing ahead of them, no red traffic light to halt them. Then they turned into a driveway she instantly recognised. Nick Sarazin's Sydney residence!

He was taking her to his home, not the Regent. He had promised Louise to keep her with him, and he was keeping his word to Justin's wife, not to her. He had lied to her again. Deceived her again. Seduced her with his pose of concern and caring.

"You have to be the most hateful man I've ever met, Nick Sarazin!" she seethed, jabbing at the seat belt release button and trying to struggle free of the rug. "I'll never believe another word you say!"

He threw her a look of soft appeal, the blue eyes as insidiously winning as she had found them last night. "I can't take you to the Regent looking as you do, Keira," he reasoned. "I will take you, I promise. After you've cleaned up."

Her heart galloped in frantic protest. She couldn't trust him. He would find another excuse and another excuse not to take her, and keep playing on the attraction he knew she felt for him. Just as he had when he'd wrapped her in the rug. It had been so weak of her to let him hold her and kiss her. Hopelessly weak!

There was only one thing to do. The moment the car stopped, Keira was out and running, hurling the rug away from her to free her legs from any constriction.

"Keira! No!" he shouted, and she heard his feet crunching the gravelled driveway as he started to run after her.

She cast a frightened look over her shoulder. She had about a five metre start on him. If she simply ran to the next house, would the people there help her? But if no-one was home...

"Colonel! Stop her!" Nick yelled.

Keira instantly swung her gaze forward, alarmed at the thought of meeting some other opposition to her leaving.

She couldn't believe her eyes.

The retired British wrestler who had sat next to her on the plane, who had saved her from Louise's clawing, was right in front of her, the huge bulk of his body blocking her way, legs and arms spread in readiness for catching her.

CHAPTER EIGHT

"You!" HE CRIED, as startled as she was.

His walrus moustache quivered. His arms dropped, his hands instinctively moving to protect himself from a repeat of his previous encounters with Keira.

Although it hadn't been her fault either time, Keira thought. She could have run past him then, but her step had faltered at being confronted with the big man.

His gaze was drawn to her breasts, still clearly outlined by the damp T-shirt. His eyes goggled for a moment before he dragged them to her face in urgent pleading. "Don't hurt me," he begged. "I've got nothing to do with it, whatever is happening."

"I'm sorry. Truly I am," Keira said sincerely. "If you'll just let me go around you..."

However, before any action could be taken, the mohair rug enveloped her again and Nick Sarazin's strong arms were around her shoulders and waist, holding her immobilised. He pinned her against his body, making her sharply aware of his powerful muscularity.

"Thanks, Colonel," he panted gratefully.

The big man's relief was enormous. He straightened to a more dignified stance, puffing his massive chest out as though he had actually done something.

"Colonel, you can't let him do this to me," Keira pleaded. "He carried me off and seduced me and—"

"No, no!" The big man firmly shook his head, then looked at her knowingly. "Mr. Sarazin wouldn't do such a thing. Something else must have happened. You're a very dangerous young woman."

"Thanks for the understanding, Colonel," Nick said with considerable relief.

"He's abducting me now," Keira explained frantically. "He's keeping me with him against my will. Please do something, Colonel."

"Keep you out of trouble," the colonel approved. "You can't walk the streets—" he harrumphed "—as you are. Not without the rug. There's no telling what might happen. Or who might get hurt. Terribly dangerous."

"I deeply appreciate your vote of confidence, Colonel," Nick said with sickening gratitude. "Maybe you can talk some sense to her. Between the two of us we might be able to convince her to be reasonable. All I want is to give her the opportunity to get cleaned up and into some fresh dry clothes so she'll look decent."

"My word, yes!" the colonel agreed with fervour. "Most essential. Too dangerous the way she is." He eyed Keira sternly. "You may not mean to cause a lot of damage, young lady, but you've got to think of others." He wagged a reproachful finger at her. "The least you can do is minimise the impact. You don't want to cause loss of life. Which is possible, looking the way you do."

"Colonel, you won't help me?" Keira pleaded.

"Not in the way you mean."

"Would you call the police?"

"Definitely not! They're very busy people and—"

"Colonel, are you staying here with him?" Keira asked anxiously, seeing one possible way out of this hopeless impasse.

"Yes, I am," he affirmed. "Mr. Sarazin has kindly offered me his hospitality. Very generously. Very generously indeed," he repeated emphatically.

"If I get cleaned up and look decent, will you make sure he lets me go?" she pleaded.

The colonel frowned, looked over her shoulder at the man holding her in tight constraint.

"I assure you, Colonel, I will take this young lady wherever she wants to go, when she's fit to be seen in public," Nick said fervently.

The colonel nodded in satisfaction and returned a stern gaze to Keira. "You have his word. Mine, too. You don't need any more than that."

"I might, Colonel," Keira said with deep feeling, her large green eyes fixed imploringly on his. "Can I trust you to keep to your word?"

His big face went bright red. "Absolutely!" He harrumphed again. "Better get moving. Can't stand out here all day."

Satisfied that she had at least won this point, Keira twisted her head around and shot Nick Sarazin a hard, bitter look. "You don't have to hold me any more. I'll come quietly. For cleaning up purposes only."

"That's all I intended, Keira," he said softly. His blue eyes apologised for the distress he had given her.

He withdrew his restraining embrace and stepped back, gesturing an invitation towards the house.

Keira felt painfully confused. Had she misjudged him? Could he be trusted now? If he had a guest in his house, he could hardly have meant to keep her at his side by force. And he must have servants, as well. At least a housekeeper for this huge residence. He had spoken to someone in his employ last night, giving instructions. She simply hadn't been thinking straight. The shock of finding herself here instead of at the Regent had completely thrown her.

A self-conscious flush heated her cheeks. "I'm sorry," she said impulsively. "I guess I was behaving like a fool."

"I should have explained better," he replied, generously taking the blame for the misunderstanding.

She searched his eyes, desperately unsure of how she felt about him. How could he have been so hard-hearted and calculating, when now he seemed genuinely kind and caring?

"I don't mean you any harm, Keira," he said softly. His mouth twisted in rueful irony. "I never did, believe it or not."

Her heart lifted immeasurably and she heard herself say, "I believe you."

He smiled a dazzling white smile that danced through her mind and her heart and her soul. "At least that's a step in the right direction," he said in a tone of deep relief and pleasure.

He *is* the one, Keira thought, then didn't know if she was going mad under the stresses of the day.

Nick gently grasped her elbow. "Come inside now. A shower to wash the sand and sea off, then a spa bath to take away all the tension, and you'll feel much more ready to face the world."

"Yes," she agreed dazedly.

"Dangerous," the colonel muttered in a tone of grim foreboding.

He was right, Keira thought, as she moved ahead at Nick's urging. She couldn't be sure Nick Sarazin hadn't simply changed tack to seduce her again, suiting his manner to the circumstances. But at least this was no longer a now-or-never situation. She could walk away from it, and if Nick genuinely wanted to pursue a relationship with her he would come after her.

As he had been doing all day, Keira suddenly realised. But there were other reasons for that, not necessarily the kind of strong attraction that never wanted to let go. When, or rather if, Louise and Justin got back together again, Keira could begin to feel more certain of what Nick Sarazin felt towards her, but she no longer thought it was quite so imperative to thrust him out of her life and shut the door on him.

He led her through the house to what she suspected was the master bedroom suite. It was too large to be a mere guest room. Besides, the royal blue and off-white and red furnishings were manly enough to indicate that this was Nick's room. A king-size bed, she noticed, and opposite the bed a large unit containing a television set and speakers for whatever music facilities were behind the cupboard doors. There was also a heap of magazines on the bedside table.

Nick did not pause in the bedroom. He opened a door that led into an incredibly spacious and luxurious bathroom, and set about turning on the taps to fill a spa bath, clearly designed to accommodate two people. Keira wondered how many women Nick Sarazin had invited to bathe with him over the years, then sternly told herself it was none of her business. Except he was certainly very skilful in the art of seduction, and she had better watch her step very carefully.

The spa had a wide marble ledge around it and Keira sat down there, watching Nick as he sprinkled bath salts into the water from an elegant onyx jar. The smell of the salts was fresh and invigorating rather than heavily perfumed. The running water turned them into a foam that looked inviting.

Nick opened a mirrored cupboard, took out a folded towelling bathrobe and a blow-drier for her hair, then laid them on the vanity bench, ready for her use. "Anything else you need?" he asked, clearly intent on pleasing her.

"A comb, please," Keira said.

He opened a drawer and added a comb to the pile. "I'll have some clothes for you by the time you're finished in here. Take as long as you like, Keira. There's no hurry, is there?" The blue eyes flashed at her in persuasive appeal.

"No. I guess not," she said uncertainly.

She was clutching the rug tightly around her, waiting for him to leave her alone. Somehow being in this bathroom with him was generating a sense of intimacy that she wasn't sure she welcomed. Nick Sarazin was too vital a man to be ignored, and she was far too aware of everything about him—the corded muscles of his bare forearms, the lithe economical way he moved, the tight springiness of his black curls, the masculinity of his buttocks, the denim of his jeans stretching tightly over powerful thighs when he bent down...

As though he sensed her unease, he flicked the switch that started the spa action in the bath, then gave her an encouraging smile. "I'll leave you to it then. Just turn that switch off before pulling the plug. Okay?"

"Okay." She gave him a somewhat shaky smile. "Thank you for looking after me, Nick."

"My pleasure," he said warmly, making a graceful exit.

It felt good to slip the gritty T-shirt and underpants off. It was even better to stand under a hot shower and wash the sand from her hair and body. She shampooed her long tresses twice to make sure all the salt water was rinsed away. Then she wrapped her hair in a towel and slid into the soft foam of the spa bath.

This was sheer heaven, she thought, as the spurts of water from the nozzles hit her skin and tingled over it. She lay back and whimsically decided she could stay here forever. The air bubbles massaged her muscles, releasing the fatigue and the aches and the pains, and Keira felt at peace with herself for the first time that day.

A knock on the door startled her into sitting up. "Who is it?" she called suspiciously.

"Mrs. Patterson. The housekeeper, dear. Mr. Sarazin thought you might like a nice cool drink while you were enjoying your bath."

"Oh yes! Thank you! Come in."

She slid her body under the bubbly foam as the door opened to reveal a middle-aged woman of plump proportions. Her pepper-and-salt hair was neatly permed. She wore a blue dress and a friendly smile on an open, friendly face. Her brown eyes twinkled curiously at Keira as she carried a tray containing a long glass of orange juice.

"This is very kind of you," Keira said to cover a sudden embarrassment at being in Nick Sarazin's bath.

"Not at all," the housekeeper demurred. "I always look after Mr. Sarazin's guests. That's part of my job. Is orange juice all right?"

"Lovely, thank you." Ice clinked in the glass as Keira lifted it off the tray. The smell of freshly squeezed oranges made Keira's mouth water. She hadn't realised how thirsty she was.

Mrs. Patterson bent and picked up the rug and the damp gritty clothes. "I'll take these out of your way," she said.

Keira flushed. "Sorry they're such a mess, Mrs. Patterson."

"So long as you're all right, dear. That's the main thing. And not to worry. Mr. Sarazin will look after you," the housekeeper admonished kindly, then bestowed another friendly smile on Keira before leaving with the bundle of washing.

It made Keira wonder what story Nick had concocted to explain her arrival in such a bedraggled state. Probably that he had saved her from drowning, she decided. A waif of the world with nowhere to go. Which was close enough to the truth. Although she didn't need Nick Sarazin to look after her. On the other hand, the idea of him looking after her permanently was definitely seductive.

Eventually Keira pulled herself out of the bath, deciding she couldn't stay there forever. She turned off the switch, lifted the plug, then dried herself thoroughly before wrapping the towel around her to form a makeshift sarong while she dried her hair.

She felt lethargic after the long bath, and her arms ached from holding the hair dryer by the time she was finished with it. However, her hair was a long, clean, gleaming mane again, spilling over her shoulders like finely spun silk. Keira put on the bathrobe, tied it securely, then ventured out to the bedroom. There were no clothes set out for her that she could see, so she decided to walk through the house until she found someone.

The colonel was seated in the large living-room, which faced onto the pool and patio. On seeing her, he rose instantly from his leather armchair and waved her to another chair on the other side of a long coffee table.

"Come sit down. I'll go and tell Mrs. Patterson you're ready," he said.

Keira did as she was bid, somewhat surprised that it was the housekeeper and not Nick Sarazin who was to be summoned to take care of her. Maybe Mrs. Patterson was preparing some clothes for her, Keira reasoned.

The colonel returned and bestowed an approving smile on her. "That's better, isn't it?" he said in an avuncular tone.

"Yes," Keira agreed. "Where's Mr. Sarazin?"

"Gone to get you some suitable clothes. Back soon," he informed her. "Mrs. Patterson is bringing us some afternoon tea. Marvellous woman, Mrs. Patterson. She understands all about afternoon tea."

He was very British, Keira thought with a little smile. "Is this your first trip to Australia, Colonel?" she asked.

"Yes. First trip. And I must speak to you about that," he said on a note of urgency. He leaned forward in his chair. "You see, British taxes are ruinous. People think I make a lot of, er, money, being who I am, but that's not so. Not so at all. Only a bit player. A small-time character actor. Nothing big. And taxes take most of it—"

"Here we are, Colonel Winton!" Mrs. Patterson announced as she wheeled in a traymobile. She beamed at the big man as she started unloading a plate of Devonshire scones and a plate of little sandwiches onto the coffee table.

"You are a treasure, Mrs. Patterson." The colonel beamed at her.

As all the tea things were set out, Keira was privately amused by the fact that she had been hopelessly wrong with her idea of the colonel being a retired wrestler. Looking at him now, she could see he would make a marvellous character actor.

As soon as the housekeeper left them, the colonel leaned forward confidentially. "I've come out here to feature in a series of TV advertisements that Mr. Sarazin wants to make. I was supposed to fly first class, but there's a big difference in the fare between first and economy classes. Thousands. So I thought I'd save the money. Taxes, you know. Very hard to get around taxes."

"Yes. I expect it is," Keira said dryly. She'd never had to worry about such a thing herself, never having flown first class and never having paid taxes, but clearly it was of great concern to the colonel.

"So I thought, just between us, you don't have to tell Mr. Sarazin that I didn't fly first class, do you? I suffered a great deal to save that money."

She gave him a sympathetic smile, remembering all too well her own suffering to save money. And she hadn't spilt boiling coffee over herself. "I promise you, I won't say a word about it, Colonel." It was the least she could do to make up for the incidents that had happened around her.

"Ah!" He beamed happily. "A remarkable young woman. Remarkable! Are you in the acting field, as well?"

"No. I'm just a travelling girl," Keira replied simply.

He looked surprised. "I thought, well, with your face and, uh, figure, and being with Mr. Sarazin..."

"That's something personal," she said dismissively.

His face went bright red again. "Oh, ah, yes, understandable, of course." He recovered from his confusion and plucked up an avuncular smile. "Beastly long flight, wasn't it?"

"It certainly was." She laughed as she added, "I thought my bottom would never recover."

"From what?" Nick Sarazin's voice inquired pleasantly from behind her.

The colonel leapt in before Keira could answer. "From sitting so long. All those hours from London. Miss... Uh, Keira and I were on the same flight out. We were commiserating with each other over the discomforts of travelling so far in one hop."

"You were on the same plane?" Nick asked, the blue eyes sharply probing Keira's as he joined them.

"Yes. I was flying economy class, which is a lot more cramping than first class," Keira said to ease the colonel's concern over a possible gaffe.

Nick frowned. "You only arrived here yesterday morning?"

She nodded. "A bit past five, wasn't it, Colonel?"

He nodded, too. "Frightful hour." He leaned forward. "Shall I pour the tea for you, my dear?"

"Thank you."

Nick placed some carrier bags on the armchair next to Keira's. "I hope something fits," he said in a distracted fashion. Then he settled on the armchair next to the colonel's so he was facing her.

Throughout afternoon tea, Keira could feel Nick reviewing everything that had happened, assessing, drawing conclusions, all from the fact that she had arrived in Australia only yesterday morning. He offered little conversation, only answering questions when asked. The blue eyes rarely strayed from Keira, and she grew more and more conscious of all the things he would be adding up in his mind. She hoped he wasn't like Justin, who added things up all the time and thought life should be answerable to numbers and logic.

What would be obvious to Nick Sarazin was the fact that she had known Justin all her life and their families had been close.

The fact that her bags had been at Justin's house.

The fact that she had been Delilah for Justin last night.

The fact that Justin owed her a payment.

Nick would undoubtedly realise that there was no affair between her and Justin, and that last night's adoration was all pretence for Louise's benefit. The act had worked only too well, resulting in consequences that were totally disproportionate to what had been a well-meant deception.

The colonel polished off a prodigious amount of scones and sandwiches, adding to his already impressive girth. Neither Nick nor Keira ate much, but nothing was left of all Mrs. Patterson had provided. The colonel rubbed his bulging stomach in blissful contentment and beamed at both Keira and Nick.

"If you two good people will excuse me, I think I'll have a little nap before dinner," he declared.

They excused him.

The tension in the room instantly rose.

Keira worried over whether Nick had reached the idea that she had set out to seduce him away from Louise at Justin's urging, and felt a yawning pit in her stomach despite the afternoon tea. If he tried justifying what he had done on that score, they had very definitely reached the end. What she had felt with him last night had nothing whatsoever to do with Justin or Louise.

If he didn't leap to conclusions, if he decided to question her or invite her to explain the situation, Keira decided she would tell him the whole truth. There was no longer any obligation to keep silent for Justin's sake. Whether Nick would understand how it had all come about was, of course, rather critical to any future relationship between them. If there was to be one. Which was still highly questionable, given his motives for seducing her.

"There is more to you than meets the eye," he said slowly, mildly, consideringly.

"Not at all," Keira defended. "What you see is what you get."

He chewed on that for a few moments.

Keira kept stewing over what he thought of her. Did he believe she was a Delilah who played fast and loose with any man she found attractive, or did he now realise that she was not given to light impulsive affairs? If she hadn't thought he was the one...

"What are you going to do after I, uh, leave you at the Regent?" he asked.

Keira's heart plummeted. He was letting her go. He didn't want to keep her any more, not for Louise's sake nor his own. He had added up the facts and decided she was no threat to Louise's marriage, that her relationship with Justin was one of old acquaintances, strictly platonic. There was no need for interference. No need for any further seduction.

Which left her to herself again.

No point in hanging around in Sydney. Justin didn't want her messing up any reconciliation he could effect with Louise. Best to make her way up the coast to Queensland, she thought dully, yet inwardly she recoiled from the prospect of having to be bright and cheerful for Auntie Joan and Uncle Bruce. She needed time to get herself together again, time to put all this behind her. Somewhere cheap where no-one would bother her.

"Have you ever heard of a place called Boomerang?" she asked, her green eyes mocking his supposed interest in her future plans.

"No. I've never heard of it," he replied.

"Never been there?"

"No."

That was good. Easier to wipe him out of her memory if they shared no ground in common. "You have no idea where it is?" she asked to make doubly sure of that.

"No."

"Then," said Keira decisively, "I think I'll go there."

The skin between Nick Sarazin's eyes furrowed as he fiercely concentrated. The pieces of the jigsaw puzzle presented by Keira were falling into place. Of course, there were a few pieces missing, but he hoped he now had most of the overall picture. If he was wrong... That didn't bear thinking about. He had been wrong too many times already today, and he had only recovered this far by the skin of his teeth. Keira was something outside his experience. One thing was certain. He couldn't afford another mistake.

"You really can't get rid of me fast enough, can you?" he probed softly.

Her chin came up. The green eyes flashed with pride. "I'm glad that perception is starting to sink in." Then with a touch of scorn to cover the hurt lurking behind it, "You're not a very fast learner, Nick."

She was right. He had let himself be blinded by Delilah and not seen Keira fast enough. There was no way he could undo the damage at this point. He knew he needed a symbol. A few of them, in fact. People always thought he was gambling when he did these sorts of things. But Nick knew he wasn't gambling for the simple reason that he always won. He crossed his fingers. I hope I'm not making the biggest mistake of my life this time, he thought. But I'm getting nowhere here. The situation has to be changed.

He rose to his feet.

"Well, if that's the case," he said agreeably, "I think I'll oblige." He gestured towards the carrier bags. "If you'll go and get changed, I'll take you to Justin. And the Regent."

He saw the shock of disbelief flash across her face. At least he had got rid of the idea he was keeping her at his side for Louise's sake, he thought with satisfaction. But the satisfaction was short-lived when he saw the sharp recoil of hurt in her eyes. His heart squeezed tight and he began to doubt the course he had set himself.

"Very well," she said and slowly, wearily, pushed herself up from the chair, her beautiful face shadowed by bleak disillusionment.

She stepped to the adjacent armchair and picked up the carrier bags without so much as a glance inside them to see what he had bought for her. She simply didn't care about such things, he thought. Totally meaningless to her. Which was something he'd never met in any other woman.

Nick had no doubt that she'd spoken the absolute truth when she'd said he couldn't buy her. There had to be another answer for the payment from Justin. She hadn't played Delilah for money. Out of friendship? Caring for his happiness? Owing him a favour? Wanting to help save his marriage?

She paused, looked up at him, her sea-green eyes luminous with the Lorelei look that swam into his soul and tugged at something there...and he had the spine-chilling sensation that a king tide was going out and he was being left behind.

The urge to wrap her in his arms and hold her tight was so strong he could barely restrain it. To do so would be wrong, very wrong. If he didn't force himself to let her go, she would never accept the trust he wanted to share with her.

"What's holding you back?" he asked, his voice harsh and rasping in his need to control the rampant desire churning through him.

The light in her eyes clicked out, replaced by a hard glitter of pride. "Nothing," she snapped. "Absolutely nothing."

She marched away from him, head high, back straight, her silken hair swishing around her shoulders.

Nick watched her until she was out of sight, fighting the desire to follow her, to take her as he had taken her last night, to share with her everything they could share until she was forced to acknowledge that nothing else mattered.

But force would never work with Keira. He knew that beyond all reasonable doubt. She was a free spirit who made her own choices. If he didn't respect that he didn't have a chance in hell. Nick Sarazin always maximised his chances. He would treat Keira differently to every other woman he had ever known.

He wandered out to the patio where he had danced with her. Was it only last night? He felt he had lived through lifetimes since then. Seeing her run into the sea as though she preferred that world to any holding him, finding her gone from the shower, trying to get her into the car, trying to get her into this house...

He shook his head.

He had to treat her differently.

The seduction of Keira required the utmost delicacy, a far more mental process than a physical one, and letting her go was the first step.

But he would get her back. He would chase her to the ends of the earth. Wherever it was necessary to go. Whatever it took. He was not going to accept "never."

CHAPTER NINE

KEIRA TIPPED THE CONTENTS of the carrier bags onto
Nick's king-size bed. A couple of expensive bras and
matching panties in silk and lace, two different sizes;
two pairs of white sandals; a tangerine gaberdine skirt
with an elasticised waist; a white crocheted top with
little tangerine knobs worked through it. The price
tags had been cut off the clothes, but Keira knew that
none of them was cheap.

She hated having to take anything from Nick Sarazin, but since it was *his* choice that she be properly
cleaned up and dressed before he took her to the Regent, she was not responsible for the expense he had
gone to. She certainly hadn't asked it of him. She
hadn't known he had meant to buy her clothes.
Something borrowed from a charity shop would have
done her just as well.

However, she had no heart for arguing the toss at
this point. The sooner she was dressed, the sooner she
could get away from him. She had been right about his
mind being alien to hers. How could she have been so
mistaken about him? At least the confusion he had
stirred was slowly clearing. There could be nothing
meaningful between them. When he dropped her off
at the Regent, that was that.

She forced herself to put on a set of the underwear he had provided, and found the process repugnant. They were the kind of things a man would give to a Delilah. Keira knew she would never wear them again. In fact, she would tear them off the moment she was safely in her room at the hotel.

She didn't mind the skirt and top so much. They didn't seem so personal. She managed to fit her feet into one pair of the sandals. They were a bit tight across the toes, but she didn't have to wear them for very long. She would take all these things to a Smith Family depot tomorrow. No doubt Nick Sarazin could afford such a donation to the poor and needy.

She left the extras on the bed and walked to the living-room, where she had left him. He was standing on the patio where they had danced together. Was it only last night? Could one come alive and die within less than twenty-four hours? She stared at him and felt a numb passivity. No hatred. No love. No passion either way. He was not the one. He was a stranger who had walked into her past and out of her future.

He turned and saw her, then walked briskly inside. "Ready?" he asked.

"Yes," she said.

Those were the only words they spoke from leaving his residence at Hunter's Hill until they arrived in the city.

Keira had never been to the Regent before. It stood in a commanding position on Circular Quay. Justin's definition of the best was not necessarily the same as everyone else's, but as Nick pulled his Jaguar to a halt in the private driveway, Keira took one look through the huge glass doors and decided Justin probably knew what he was talking about this time. The luxurious foyer spelled class with a capital C.

She could now understand Nick's reservations about delivering her here in her former state. Not that she would have cared. She could have weathered a few lifted eyebrows with no trouble at all. Too many people lived their lives by what others might think of them. That was not for her. She knew what she was inside and she was comfortable with herself. That counted for more than what others might think. If Nick Sarazin didn't care for how she thought or what she was, they were better apart.

She released her seat belt as he switched off the engine. She looked directly at him and said, "Thank you. Goodbye and good luck, Nick." Her hand was already opening her door so that he need not get out at all.

"I'm coming inside with you, Keira," he stated decisively. "I want to be certain you are safely looked after."

She threw him a hard, cold look. "I don't need you looking after me."

He returned a look of grim determination. "For my own peace of mind."

Keira paused to consider that. Maybe he did have a conscience, which was giving him considerable unease. She looked away. He opened his door and slid out, cutting off any further argument.

With a vexed sigh of resignation, Keira alighted from the car and resolutely ignored Nick Sarazin's presence beside her as he accompanied her into the hotel. She did not pause to appreciate the marvellous ambience of the foyer, which rose to the height of three podium levels. Having to postpone the moment of farewell made her feel uneasy. Nick Sarazin liked having his own way too darned much. She marched straight to the inquiry desk. Thankfully, a member of the staff gave her instant attention.

"How can I help you, ma'am?"

"Mr. Justin Brooks was to book a room for me here. Could you please check to see if he's done that?"

"Was the room to be in his name or yours, ma'am?"

"I don't know."

"Your name, ma'am?"

"Keira Mary Brooks," she said with a touch of defiance, conscious that Nick was listening.

The desk attendant smiled. "I'll check the computer."

If Nick Sarazin showed any reaction to her full name, Keira did not see it. She kept her gaze fastened on the desk attendant, who quickly confirmed that the booking had been made.

"Can you please check if my bags have arrived?" Keira asked.

"Certainly, ma'am. Just a few moments while I call the baggage room."

Keira steeled herself to turn and face Nick for the last time. His face was stamped with grim determination, yet the blue eyes seemed to have a sick, hungry look as they met hers. She wasn't sure if it was her tension or his that made it difficult to speak, but she finally forced the necessary words out.

"You can go with complete peace of mind now, Nick."

His mouth twisted into an ironic smile. "Oh, I wouldn't say that, Keira. I'll let you go. That was my promise. Try to keep out of trouble."

"I'll be fine, thank you," she said stiffly. Without him she wouldn't have *been* in any trouble, and her eyes mockingly told him that.

"I hope so," he said softly and turned away. He moved a few paces, then swung around, the blue eyes stabbing at her. "You really did play me for being a dummy, didn't you, Keira Mary Brooks?"

"Don't be a fool, Nick," she answered softly, her heart and soul suddenly throbbing the message that this was a man she could have loved forever, if his mind had been more in tune with hers. "Even though I was under a promise of silence, I didn't once lie to you. It's not my fault that you couldn't recognise truth," she added sadly.

His eyes lingered on her, sweeping over her in one final glance before he turned away again. He took a step, then ran straight into Justin.

"I want a word with you, Sarazin," Justin said in a low, threatening voice. "A lot of words."

His face was flushed with anger. His body projected the fact that he was in a fighting mood—legs slightly apart, chest puffed out, hands clenched, shoulders squared, chin out, mouth grim, brown eyes blazing.

On the other hand, Nick's tension of a few moments ago instantly relaxed into a non-threatening pose. "Go right ahead, Mr. Brooks. I am fascinated to hear what you have to say," he drawled.

"I want to know what you did to Keira," Justin demanded. "As far as I'm concerned, she's my *sister.*"

"Your sister?"

"As good as," Justin declared vehemently. "Keira has been in our family since she was ten. We're close. Very close. I've always regarded her as my little sister." He raised a hand and poked a finger in Nick Sarazin's chest as he added, "And you made her cry!"

Keira was so astonished at this big-brotherly display from her cousin that she simply stood riveted to the spot, seeing Justin in a totally new light.

"Feeling a bit guilty about your part in this, are you, Mr. Brooks?" Nick taunted softly.

Of course, thought Keira. That accounted for at least some of Justin's aggression. But all the same, he was family sticking up for family, and Keira felt fonder of her cousin in that moment than she had ever done before.

Justin's face went a darker red. "A man has a right to save his marriage. Any way he can. Particularly from people like you. You tried to do the wrong thing by Louise. You did the wrong thing by Keira...."

"Oh, hell!" Nick Sarazin groaned, a look of anguish on his face. His misdeeds were obviously getting the better of him.

Justin's finger poked again. "Now that you've failed with Keira, don't think you can come back to Louise. If you try that..." He looked Nick Sarazin up and down, saw the difference in physique, knew he was at a disadvantage, but went on. "If you so much as look at Louise again, I'll knock the brains out of your head!''

"No need for that," Nick retorted coolly. "I have never had anything but a friendly and professional relationship with Louise. Never intended anything else. I'm sorry that things have worked out the way they have. Might I recommend that you and your wife sit down and talk to each other, instead of involving other people in your stupid games.''

"Games!" Justin said scathingly. "Who started it, eh? Who went on with it last night and hurt Keira so much she cried?''

"I've had nothing whatsoever to do with the dispute between Louise and yourself, Mr. Brooks," Nick replied in a calm, soothing voice. "I wanted to talk to you about that last night. Louise has been very wrong and very foolish to use me as a tool in her argument with you. I want that cleared up.''

"Oh yeah," Justin jeered disbelievingly.

"Yes!" Nick affirmed. "It was you who upset the apple cart. You chose to turn up with your Delilah, which turned Louise into a hysterical madwoman. I might add that my perception of Keira was influenced by the fact that she was with a married man. Which was your fault, my friend.''

"Oh, sure!" Justin's mouth curled in contempt. "Everything is someone else's fault! Everybody blames me, including Louise. A very convenient shifting of cause and effect so that you don't have to feel responsible for anything." His fists balled. "I ought to smash your face in.''

"Do so, if it makes you feel better," Nick said flatly. "I'm well aware that I should have treated Keira differently. That blame is certainly mine."

Justin glared black murder at him. "You and your playboy games! I've never known Keira to cry before in her life. She breezes through everything. But you had to do it, didn't you? You had to carry her off and have your way with her. In the old days they had it right. You ought to be made to marry her—"

"Justin," Keira protested sharply. Then in a quiet appeasing tone, she added, "I did go willingly. I thought..." She flushed painfully. "Never mind what I thought. It's over now. Please let Mr. Sarazin go, Justin. There's no point in this."

"He shouldn't be allowed to get away with it," Justin argued. "Shotguns," he added fiercely. "That's what we need. Plenty of shotguns."

"If it's any satisfaction to you, Mr. Brooks, I didn't enjoy making Keira cry," Nick said in a tone of quiet sincerity. "I regret it very deeply. I've done all she would let me do to make amends. I would suggest that you stop haranguing me and start taking care of her."

Justin's brow furrowed in concern as his eyes darted over her. "What can I do, Keira?" he asked.

"I'd like to go to my room," she said wearily.

"Right!" he agreed, the steam going out of him as he looked fretfully at her. "I'll get the key and take you up." Then he cast Nick one last belligerent look. "You keep out of our family, Nick Sarazin. I've had enough of your interfering ways!"

"Mr. Brooks—" Nick's voice dropped to a low note of urgency "—make sure Keira has everything she needs. She won't take any more from me."

"Neither she should!" Justin rushed out angrily. "I'll look after her."

Nick's hand shot out and squeezed his arm. "Take good care of her!"

The action and the delivery of those words carried an ominous threat. Keira couldn't see Nick's face, but his body suddenly looked as tense as a coiled spring. Justin looked startled, but before he could react, Nick removed his grasp and strode away without a backwards glance.

Justin stared after him with a dark frown on his face, shook his head, then came over to Keira, his brow still puckered in thought. "That guy didn't want to let you go, Keira."

"You made him feel guilty. That's all, Justin," she said dispiritedly. "Let's move. Since you're here, I'd like to talk to you. In private."

"Of course," he agreed, his eyes searching hers in a troubled fashion. "Did he hurt you physically, Keira?"

"No." A sadly ironic smile curved her lips. "He actually looked after me very-well once he accepted that I wouldn't stay with him."

Justin cleared his throat and looked relieved. "That's all right then," he muttered, then stepped over to the desk and took charge of getting her and her bags to the suite he had booked.

A porter accompanied them to demonstrate all the features and facilities for guests' enjoyment and comfort in the apartment, which he called an executive suite. It comprised a bedroom, lounge and dining-area, plus a luxurious bathroom. He opened the curtains along two walls to reveal a magnificent view of Sydney Harbour, pointed out the telescope in the corner for more detailed viewing, explained how to operate the television, the lights and the telephone, wished Keira a pleasant stay and finally departed.

"This must be costing a fortune, Justin," she remarked ruefully, sinking into one of the leather lounges.

He shrugged and slanted her an apologetic smile. "I'm sorry I got you into this, Keira. If I'd had any idea that Sarazin wasn't genuinely taken with you, I would have told you about his connection with Louise. But the way he looked at you..." He heaved a deep sigh and settled onto the opposite lounge.

Keira didn't want to talk about Nick Sarazin. That episode was closed, as far as she was concerned. "Have you told Louise about me yet?" she asked.

Justin frowned. "I planned on doing that tonight. I hadn't figured on this happening. Do you think Sarazin will tell her before I do?"

"No. I think he's wiped his hands of the whole affair. But, Justin, it must be obvious to you now that Louise loves you very much and doesn't want any other woman to have her husband. She didn't leave you for another man," Keira said pointedly. "There's something else behind this. What's actually going on?"

Justin's face took on a sullen look. "It's time we started a family. I'm thirty, you know. I don't want to be an old father."

Typical Justin, Keira thought. Life by numbers. "Doesn't Louise want to have a baby?" she asked softly.

"She agreed about having a family before we were married," Justin argued, looking even more sullen. "Four years I've waited. That's long enough. And now that she's finally pregnant, she says she's going to abort the baby. My child!" He rose to his feet in towering outrage, gesticulating his disgust. "Just because she reckons she's not ready, she wants to get rid of our child! No way in the world am I going to go along with that!"

Keira was shocked that Louise would even suggest such a thing. She couldn't imagine wanting to get rid of a child conceived by a loved husband. It felt all wrong. "Why did Louise let herself get pregnant if she wasn't ready?" she asked, trying to understand why this was happening.

A guilty flush darkened Justin's face. He avoided Keira's questioning eyes. He made an awkward dismissive gesture. "Louise kept putting it off and putting it off. I, uh, mucked up the contraceptive thing. I thought if she happened to get pregnant she would accept it and we wouldn't be arguing about it anymore. As it turned out, that wasn't one of my best ideas."

Men! Keira was swamped by a wave of resentment. Why did they think they had a God-given right to take free choice from women? Blindly intent on having their own way no matter what!

Having suffered through Nick Sarazin's bullying, Keira found herself a lot more sympathetic towards Louise's cause, although she still couldn't sympathise with the idea of an abortion. She took a deep breath and tried to talk calmly about a woman's point of view.

"Justin, Louise is the one who has to bear the pregnancy. And all the changes it will make to her. A baby doesn't interfere much with a man's life-style, but if Louise enjoys her job and her freedom ..."

"Keira, we agreed on having a family!" Justin justified himself strongly. "I'm not asking for a whole brood of kids. Only two. Preferably a boy and a girl. I'm trying to organise that. Now surely that's not too much to ask of the woman I've married. The woman I want to have my kids. She said she wanted them, too."

"All right," Keira soothed. "So the deed is done and Louise is pregnant, and she found out you tricked her into it."

"She's twenty-eight, for heaven's sake!" Justin cried in exasperation. "Statistics say that a woman has a better chance of having healthy babies before she's thirty. After thirty, the percentages start going against you. That's the figures, no matter how you look at them."

Numbers again, Keira thought with a heavy sigh. And outdated attitudes. These days women in their thirties were having perfectly healthy babies. She took another deep breath and tried getting down to the nitty-gritty of the situation. "In any event, Louise is now pregnant, and you want her to come home to you and have the baby," she stated slowly.

"Yes!" Justin affirmed. "But she's fighting mad, saying I had no right to abrogate her rights. She uses a lot of other fancy words, as well. And she said she would find another man who respects her and her rights."

"She doesn't really want someone else, Justin," Keira assured him. "You've got to start giving her a lot of extra considerations since you've forced this baby on her. If you want her back and you want the baby, why don't you offer to hire a nanny so that Louise can keep working if she wants to? If Louise has a solid career going for her, she must earn more than you'd have to pay a nanny, so you'd certainly be able to afford it."

He looked disgruntled. "Why can't she be content to stay home and be a proper mother to our child?"

"Justin, you can't have everything your own way," Keira said sternly. "It's not fair on Louise. If that isn't her choice, you can't force it. You're in this situation because you tried forcing. Doesn't that teach you something?"

She paused to let that sink in, then added, "As it is, Louise's hormones are probably all upset from being pregnant. You should be cossetting her and looking after her. Enveloping her in love. Wooing her all over again. She's the one who's making the sacrifices to have your child. You have to make it worthwhile for her. And that's going to take a lot of loving and indulgence from you. Particularly in the circumstances."

He paced up and down, chewing over that advice as though it was sour to his taste. Eventually he seemed to swallow it. "You could be right, Keira. A nanny," he said consideringly.

"Yes. And a promise that you will share in all the chores related to having a baby and not leave everything to Louise."

"Won't a nanny do that?" he asked.

"Nannies do have days off, Justin," Keira pointed out.

"Oh! Right!"

"And make a big fuss of Louise while she's pregnant. Give her flowers. Take her out a lot. Assure her that's she's still desirable to you when she starts to lose her figure. A lot of women feel very insecure about that. You've got to show her you love her all the more for carrying your child."

"Mmm . . ." He beetled a frown at Keira. "How do you know all these things? You've never had a baby." His eyes suddenly widened as an idea struck him. "Or have you? Is that why you stayed away—"

"No, Justin." She rolled her eyes in exasperation. "I was travelling around. That's all. But I have worked as a nanny and I know about pregnant women. Believe me, you're going the wrong way about this if you want to keep Louise and keep her happy. Stop talking about your rights and start working on solutions."

He grimaced, but he looked ready to start making concessions. "So you think if I take her out and give her flowers and promise her a nanny that—"

"It would be a start in the right direction. But you've also got to tell Louise about me, Justin. Tonight. Without delay. You've made her feel very insecure about you. You won't get anywhere until she feels secure again. Tell her you did it in desperation because you love her so much and you were out of your mind."

He looked affronted. "I was not out of my mind. It was a perfectly planned military operation to make her jealous."

"Well, you certainly succeeded," Keira said bitterly. "And your ignorant private soldier paid the penalty for it."

His affront crumpled into acute discomfort. "Things didn't work out exactly as I planned, Keira."

"Just get it sorted out with Louise. Tonight!" Keira demanded.

"I will. I swear I will. I'll do all you say. See if it works. There might be something in your ideas."

"Don't expect instant miracles," Keira said dryly. "You've got a lot of making up to do. The trouble with men is they don't know how to think like women. It's a dreadful fault."

"Well, how can men think like women?" Justin argued with perfect logic. "If they did that, they wouldn't be men."

This sounded like a circular argument. "You could try listening with an open mind," Keira said pointedly.

Justin wasn't listening any more, Keira thought. His eyes were boring into her from underneath another beetling frown. "I know how men think," he said triumphantly.

"Yes, I suppose you do," Keira answered wearily.

"Do you know what I think?"

"No."

"Louise asked Nick Sarazin to get you out of the way, Keira, but that's not why he did what he did. Nor why he wanted to keep you with him. He was well and truly gone on you last night. Stricken is how I describe it. Lovesick. Call it what you will. When he left us down in the foyer it was perfectly plain to me that he was still carrying a torch for you."

She threw him a pained look. "Justin, I'd prefer not to talk about—"

"Okay," he agreed soothingly. "You're probably well rid of him anyway. It's just that I know how men think."

"You may be right," she said cynically. She didn't believe him. Easy come, easy go.

He glanced at his watch. "I'd better get going. Got to buy some roses. How many?"

"I think twelve is a good number," Keira said helpfully.

"Yes. Twelve. Will you be okay, Keira? Got everything you need? I have to move fast. Get Louise back into a state of matrimonial bliss."

"Yes, do that, Justin." She gave him a grateful smile and gestured around her. "Thanks for the suite. I don't know what I would've done without you."

He responded with a funny self-conscious smile. "Well, hell! You are my little sister. Not that you ever needed me around. And you're a holy terror to pin down to anything. The way your mind works is totally unfathomable.''

"But I'm family," she finished for him. "And you're family to me, Justin. I may not seem to need you, or appreciate you, but it's always been comforting to know that you *are* around if I do need you. And not because I always need you for a loan. I truly am sorry I missed your wedding. I would have come . . .''

"Oh, I guess I only wanted to show you off to Louise," he said, good-naturedly shrugging off the grudge. "After all, not everyone has a beautiful eccentric cousin who runs off with sheikhs and leaves trails of devastation behind her."

"Trails of devastation? How can you say that? I never have! I do not!''

"Oh no?" His mouth quirked into a teasing grin. "I reckon you've caused more accidents than any other hundred women put together. Just by being you. I remember kids on bikes having all sorts of smashes because they were gawking at you. And that was when you were only a teenager. I bet you've left havoc all around the world. It's a wonder you haven't been sued for being a public nuisance."

"Justin!" she protested disbelievingly. "It's not like that. I haven't done anything."

"You don't have to. But I know why Louise wanted to tear your hair out. It's a lethal weapon. Not to mention a few other weapons in your armoury. In short, I have no trouble believing that Nick Sarazin would fight like hell to keep you. But I won't talk any more about him. You obviously don't want to talk about him."

"No. And you'd better start treating Louise right," she reminded him tersely.

"I'm going. I'll ring you in the morning with the news."

"Good luck, Justin. And do try listening," she urged, wanting everything to work out for both him and Louise.

"Thanks, Keira. And try being good for once," he admonished. "Don't go wandering off until I call you."

In a sudden rush of affection for her absurdly number-minded, but reliable cousin, Keira rose from the lounge and pressed a warm sisterly kiss on his cheek. Justin's face turned red again. She thought she heard him mutter, "Dangerous," as he hurriedly let himself out of the suite.

Keira relaxed onto the soft cushions, idly drinking in the panoramic view of Sydney Harbour. There was no other place in the world like this, she thought. Her memory clicked through a host of sights she had enjoyed and marvelled at, but this was home, and perhaps that was what made it so special to her.

Her mind drifted over the years she had been away, the countries she had travelled through, the people she had met, the friends she had made. Much of what she had seen and done had been shared with others, but no one person had shared everything with her. She wished...

She closed her eyes and the image of Nick Sarazin was sharp in her mind. Her heart clenched. Her soul cried out in yearning. Why couldn't he have been the one? It wasn't fair that they had seemed so close last night. It wasn't fair that she had felt so sure.

A sense of terrible loneliness crept through her. Maybe she would never meet the one. Maybe she was destined to always be a traveller through life, alone, never sharing with one particular person above all others, never doing everything with one constant soul mate.

That appeared to be an unattainable dream.

CHAPTER TEN

NICK SARAZIN sat on the beach at Boomerang, forearms propped listlessly on his knees, the lowering afternoon sun beating warmly on his bare back. He
stared out to sea, wondering if Keira had deliberately
misled him about coming here.

Another day almost gone and she hadn't arrived. It
was a week since he had left her at the Regent Hotel.
Seven days of waiting and watching out for her, and
God knows how many hours of worrying over what
might have happened to her in the meantime. His
hands clenched in a spasm of frustration. He
shouldn't have let her go.

What other choice did he have? his mind taunted,
and the answer came back—none that was viable! He
forced himself to relax again. She would come, he told
himself for the umpteenth time. He remembered the
bitter satisfaction in her eyes when he had confirmed
he didn't know where Boomerang was and had never
been there. She wanted somewhere totally free of him.
Therefore she would come. It was simply a matter of
waiting out the interim.

Maybe she had been caught up in the battle between Justin and Louise, and that was holding her up.
Maybe he should have stayed in Sydney and kept a

watch on things there. He shook his head, vexed at himself for indulging in purposeless speculation. He had decided on a course and he would stick it out for at least another week before reviewing what he should do.

If he hadn't come ahead of her, he wouldn't have been able to scout out the situation and set up his best chances. Paying the rent on the caravan next to his and wording up the park manager ensured that Keira would be placed where he wanted her. Close to him. And he now knew all the best places to take her. If he could persuade her into accepting his company.

There were a lot of ifs in his scenario, Nick acknowledged with a sense of barely controlled impatience. He craved action. He needed reactions to hit off so he could manoeuvre—tell her the things she needed to be told. It was this damnable waiting that was driving him around the bend.

He pushed himself up, brushed the sand off his board shorts, then tramped up over the dune to the national park, which was basically all Boomerang was. It hadn't been hard to find, nor hard to get to. When Keira had flung the name Boomerang at him, he had imagined it would probably be some tiny settlement in the Red Centre of Australia. A national park on the north coast of New South Wales had come as a pleasant surprise.

Certainly it was a long way from being a flourishing tourist resort. The place was little more than a camping site, a dozen caravans, a general store, bushland and beach. Primitive and peaceful.

Except Keira's non-appearance was nagging away at any peace that Nick might have found here.

He trudged towards the shower block, pausing now and then to exchange small talk with a few of the campers. There was no formality about Boomerang. People chatted to each other and casually invited anyone to join in activities. On the other hand, if you wanted to be left alone, you were left alone.

Out of habit and hope, but not with any real expectation, his gaze automatically swept up the road that led down to the park. A hiker was coming around the last bend, backpack strapped on, duffle bag hanging from the shoulder, a khaki cloth army hat dipping over the forehead, blue and green checked shirt hanging loose, faded jeans, army boots.

Definitely not Keira, he thought with a stab of disappointment, yet there was something about the hiker that kept him watching—the easy fluidity of movement, a kind of jauntiness that suggested pleasure in walking, a lithe roll of the hips above long shapely legs.

His heart suddenly catapulted into a wild thumping.

A thick flaxen plait hung over one shoulder.

Not even the loose shirt could fully hide the provocative jiggle of full feminine breasts.

He wanted to laugh. He wanted to shout for joy. He wanted to dash up the road and swing her into his arms and never let her go again.

Better judgement prevailed.

Nick headed for his caravan, happily secure in the knowledge that he had not waited in vain.

IT HADN'T CHANGED AT ALL, Keira thought with a surge of pleasure. Of course, Boomerang was off the general tourist track, and the five kilometres of road from Foster were so steep and winding that few motorists would bother taking that particular drive, which was little short of dangerous.

Quite a few tents were pitched in the park but it was far from crowded with campers. Enough for some company if she felt like it. The easy camaraderie at Boomerang was one of its attractions to Keira. Several people gave her a friendly wave of welcome as the manager showed her to the caravan she had rented for a week. Even the rental had remained relatively reasonable compared to what she had paid six years ago. In a way, it was like stepping into the past.

A shower first, she thought, once the manager had left her to her own devices. She laid her bags on one of the bunks, tossed her hat on another, then sat down on the double bed to remove her boots. She eased her feet out of them. Then there was a knock on her door. Some friendly soul come to offer her something, she thought with a smile. Maybe a freshly caught fish for her dinner. People were like that at Boomerang.

The smile was still lingering on her lips as she went to greet her visitor. She opened the door and there he was, blue eyes twinkling at her, blue eyes dancing through her brain, tripping her heart, sending a zing of excitement through her veins.

He offered her a long glass of orange juice that tinkled with ice. "I thought you might be thirsty," he said, flashing his dazzling white smile. "And I wanted to say hello to the woman I've been waiting for all week."

She shook her head dazedly. A thousand questions pummelled her mind. One found its way to her tongue and spilled from her lips. "Why?"

"A chance to begin again," he said softly. "Without any misconceptions this time." He nodded to the next caravan. "I'm over there. We have barbecue facilities between our separate accommodations. Will you have dinner with me this evening if I cook it for you?"

Keira was plunged into utter confusion, mental, emotional and physical. She had not expected to see Nick Sarazin ever again. All week she had been trying to bury the memory of him, filling her mind with other things, keeping herself as busy as she could. Yet his impact on her a few seconds ago had been exactly the same as when she had first seen him, despite all that had happened between them.

She took the cold drink he had brought her as she struggled to get her thoughts into some sort of coherent pattern. "Thank you," she said huskily. Her throat had gone very dry.

"Does that mean my invitation is accepted?" he asked lightly. "I'm very good at barbecues. I can cook you a fine steak, tomato, onions, bacon, banana, pineapple. I'll toss in a side salad of greens. Bought some fresh bread buns, too. How does that sound?"

His vitality swamped her with tingling life. Keira found it impossible to reject him. "It sounds...good," she said, uncertain of any ground with him.

Justin had been right, she thought. Nick hadn't wanted to let her go. But where did he see this leading to? Another seduction that went his way? Whatever his aim was, he had to be very determined about it to have come here and waited for her all week.

"I know you'll want to unpack and get yourself settled," he said quickly. "Come and join me when you're ready."

Keira didn't know if she would ever be ready. "That would be fine," she heard herself agree.

His grin of delight sent a shaft of warmth right down to her toes. "I'll do my best to please," he said, then raised his hand in a friendly salute and left her to return to his caravan.

Keira stared after him, still struggling with a sense of disbelief. He wore a pair of brilliant orange board shorts, topped by a loose royal blue singlet which had an orange sunset above purple waves printed on the back of it. He was bare-armed, bare-legged, bare-footed, and in the casual surfie gear he could have been a beach bum. Certainly he didn't look out of place at Boomerang. Yet somehow he still retained the air that said the world was his oyster. Which he could open when he willed, and consume at his leisure.

There was a buoyancy in his step, a firm assurance in his powerfully muscled legs, a confident strength in his broad shoulders, and the curly black head seemed to be tilted high as though nothing could ever bow him down. He could go anywhere, do anything, be anything he wanted to be.

The desire to have a man like him walking beside her for the rest of her life ripped through Keira with devastating force. It shook her so much she hastily closed her door, shutting out the sight of him, trying to shut out the needs that Nick Sarazin evoked. Didn't she know that he couldn't be trusted?

Yet that wasn't entirely true, Keira amended quickly. Nick had kept his word about taking her to the Regent, and she could hardly complain about his kindness and consideration for her needs once he had given his word. In hindsight, he had been very good to her. And generous.

She took a sip of the chilled orange juice. It was delicious. A thoughtful and generous gesture, Keira acknowledged, as was his offer to cook dinner for her. She suddenly recalled Colonel Winton's enthusiastic praise of Nick's generous hospitality. It had to be part of his nature, not simply an act put on to influence her opinion of him.

If she let herself think about it, Nick Sarazin had been a very generous lover, as well. Not selfishly demanding or uncaring of her pleasure. He had made it beautiful for her. More beautiful than she could ever have imagined any man making love to her.

If Justin was right, if the seduction had had nothing whatsoever to do with Louise's request, if it was because Nick had truly fallen in love at first sight, as she had with him, then maybe he was the one after all.

After the strain of battling to put Nick Sarazin behind her, the enormity of this thought and what it might mean to her set off a trembling reaction. She almost spilled the drink in her hand. Keira set the glass down on the small dining table and slid herself onto the nearest bench seat.

A memory sliced into her mind, something Nick had said as they lay together under the stars. *Perhaps all the rest is irrelevant. It is only you that matters.* If that had been his feeling then, his true feeling, then surely there was a very real chance that this could be a new beginning.

A surge of wild happiness made Keira feel positively dizzy. She finished the drink Nick had given her, tried to steady the extremes of emotion that could lead her astray. Hope and desire did not constitute the most sensible approach to a man like Nick Sarazin.

The wisest course was to keep her distance, take the time to feel her way with Nick, make sure he was the one she wanted him to be. This evening's date with him was not a now-or-never situation. It was simply an opportunity to explore the possibilities of a new beginning.

Keira held on to this common-sense thinking right up until six o'clock. It did not stop her from fossicking through her bags for her best pair of shorts—which were a practical sage-green—and the matching shirt that tied at her waist. Nor did it quell a rush of very physical memories while she soaped her body clean in the shower. Nor did it have any influence whatsoever on her decision to unplait her hair and brush it into a free-flowing mass of crinkly waves. Nor did it assert any control over the excitement throbbing through her heart.

It was common-sense thinking that said it was silly to hang around inside in her caravan when she could be helping Nick set up for the barbecue. She could hear him outside, getting the fire going under the hot-plate, whistling to himself. A happy smile curved her lips as she recognised the tune—"Amazing Grace."

She opened her door and stepped onto the small patio. "Do you play the bagpipes, too?" she asked laughingly.

He threw her a grin, which promptly died on his face. He stared at her for several long nerve-tingling moments, and Keira felt he was absorbing every detail of her reality, savouring it as though he had hungered for it too long. Her own light-hearted amusement died under the intensity of his gaze and she was conscious only of the thunderous beat of her heart. She saw him drag in a quick breath and slowly release it. Then he stretched his mouth into the grin he had lost.

"I'll do anything you want," he said softly.

Keira felt the tug at her heart. It was the same feeling as when they had first met, the force of an inevitable attraction pulsating magnetically between them.

"My judgement of you was wrong," he said even more softly.

Keira felt the pain and the pride behind that admission. She heard the sincerity behind the words. "I made mistakes, too," she said huskily.

Her feet were tumbling off the patio, propelling her towards him. Somehow—Keira had no real awareness of how it happened—she was inside the circle of his arms and he was hugging her against his chest in a very possessive fashion. An excitingly possessive fashion. She felt his breath waft warmly through her hair and could not repress an impulsive urge to bite his shoulder.

"I don't think I like you, Nick Sarazin," she mused in a muddled-up sense of positive desire and caution.

"Forget what happened in the past," he murmured, the low throb of his voice intensely persuasive. "From the moment I first saw you, you were *the one*. No-one else. You know it. I know it. That's how it happened."

"Louise..."

"Forget Louise. She had nothing to do with it. You were *the one*."

Keira's heart skittered around her body and came to rest somewhere in the vicinity of her throat. She looked at this man, her eyes glowing in the soft light of the setting sun. So much a stranger, so much *her man*.

"Are you speaking the truth, Nick Sarazin?"

"As true as Tara," he said enigmatically, but the blue eyes were alight with a blaze of convincing fervour. "As true as my mother gave birth to me. As true as... you're Keira. *My* Keira."

"I was the one for you?" Keira asked. Her voice was way off key because of the choking position of her heart.

"You were *the one!*"

"You really felt that?"

"I swear it. From the moment I first saw you," he affirmed with passionate emphasis.

Her heart danced to its proper place, having made up its mind about how matters stood. However, the brain in Keira's head dictated that she should still have doubts about where all this was leading. Her brain dictated that she shouldn't be so easy to get this time, after all the bad things he had thought about her.

"I'm glad you said that," her heart declared. Her mind then added, "I might be able to find it in my heart to forgive you. Someday."

He pressed her closer, using the persuasive power of his aggressive maleness to instantly evoke a flood of awareness that shook the female core of Keira to her tiniest bones. With the skill of an artist who knew the value of contrast, he spent tender little kisses over her hair.

"You'll forgive me," he said softly. "I'm sure of that."

"Why should I?" She didn't want him to be too sure of her or too sure of having his own way with her. It might make him demanding.

"Because you're you," he replied huskily. He lifted her chin and planted floating kisses over her lips, punctuating a few more reasons. "Because you're a warm person, a loving person, a concerned person, and most of all a caring person. You have a giving heart, Keira. You are a loving woman. A jewel. You're the woman I want in my life."

That all sounded wonderful, but how could he know those things about her? Maybe he was just making them up to seduce her with words. "You're an ensnarer of women, Nick Sarazin," she said, letting him know he had a bit of proving to do.

"Only for you, my darling."

He scooped her up in his arms, cradling her tightly against his chest. This is getting to be a habit, Keira thought, but since it was a great improvement on being slung over his shoulder, and she secretly liked him showing her how strong he was, she let him have his way.

Before she knew it, her arms were wound around his neck—without shame or pride, she thought—and her face was so close to his throat that she had an irresistible urge to press her lips to it. Which she did. And it was very satisfying.

In case he became too encouraged, she warned him, "Forgiveness is not an easy business."

"I know," he replied with suitable solemnity. "Which is why I have to show you what I feel so it will become easier."

"How are you going to do that?" she asked suspiciously. He was carrying her towards his caravan. She could get into big trouble there if she wasn't careful.

"A surprise," he said, smiling at her so warmly and lovingly that he was at the caravan door before Keira gathered some wits.

"What surprise?" she demanded, but somehow the demand turned into an excited purr of anticipation. Bodies were terribly treacherous things, she thought.

"Close your eyes." He closed them himself with soft butterfly kisses on her eyelids.

Negotiating the step into the caravan and through the doorway was not an easy task with her in his arms. Keira helped by pressing herself as close to him as she could. There was something intensely satisfying about feeling her breasts squash into the hard, warm wall of Nick's chest. They tingled with delicious sensitivity.

The door banged shut behind them. "Am I allowed to open my eyes now?" Keira asked, an irrepressible smile on her lips. She already knew what the surprise was from the fragrance around her.

"Not yet." He carried her to the double bed and gently laid her on it. "Now!" he commanded.

The caravan was festooned with flowers of every conceivable kind. Wildflowers from the Australian bush, exotic flowers from the tropics, hothouse roses, orchids. Keira gazed around in heart-pounding wonderment, then finally plucked up the courage to meet and question the blue eyes that she knew had never left her face, blue eyes dark with need, hungry for all she could give him.

"Why, Nick?" she asked softly. "Why did you do this?"

"Because you're my flower girl," he answered simply. "Every moment of every day I thought of you, I thought of flowers. I had to have flowers in case you came. All my life I've been growing towards something, a branch out here or there, each year a fresh lead, but never feeling complete, always some part further to grow—until I met you. Then I knew, Keira. You were the bloom that had been missing, the flower I'd been growing towards, the fragrance of my life."

His words were a sweet caress on her soul, a seductive balm to the doubts that fretted her mind, a velvet glove squeezing her heart. They wound around her, through her, and Keira's free spirit suddenly quivered in a weird little panic at the sense of being shackled to him before she was ready, before she was sure that this was what she wanted, before she knew beyond all reasonable doubt that it was right.

Instinctively she sought delay, wrenching her eyes from his and sending them around the flowers again. "How on earth did you get them?" she asked.

"I went in to Forster and bought every flower they had. I had them imported. I went into the national park for the wildflowers, and every time I picked one of them, I said to myself, this is for Keira...."

Every word he spoke seemed to tighten a hoop around her chest. He sat down beside her, hemming her in on the bed, his hand reaching out to fan the long tresses of her hair out on the pillow. She tried to lighten the atmosphere, tried to smile at him teasingly.

"Oh, Nick! I hope it didn't make you feel unmanly being seen to pick flowers."

The blue eyes bathed her in love. "Not when they were for you, my darling. Why on earth should I feel *unmanly* when I'm doing something for you?"

The hoop squeezed even tighter. Keira scooped in a deep breath. Her eyes accused him of deliberate, knowing, tactically perfect ensnarement, but somehow she couldn't drive much conviction into her voice. "You're a terrible man, Nick Sarazin."

"Yes," he admitted.

She sighed. "I think I'm weakening."

"I hope so." He moved his legs onto the bed and rolled his body next to hers.

Keira's heart leapt into her throat again. "Aren't we supposed to be cooking a barbecue?" It was a ragged little protest, without any fire at all. There was a terrible amount of weakening going on inside her.

"This could be more important," he murmured, reaching across her to pluck a flower from the far pillow. It was a frangipani bloom. He gently stroked the velvet petals down her cheek.

"I am the one, aren't I, Nick?" Even Keira could hear the fear of the empty void in her voice, the black chasm that would open and swallow her up if he was deceiving her.

The blue eyes met hers with searing intensity, intent on burning away any last lingering doubt. "You're *the one,*" he assured her, his voice deep and vibrant with passion. He tucked the sweet creamy flower behind her ear. "Remember, forever, the fragrance of love," he murmured, his lips brushing softly over hers.

"Promise me, no deceit, ever," she whispered, barely stopping her lips from clinging sensuously to his.

"I love you," he promised and showed her, with his mouth and his hands and his body, how very much and in how many ways he loved her, and Keira surrendered to the passion of his embrace, surrendered herself into his possession, and came once more into the sweet valley that was so full of warm blissful sunshine, a valley of glorious contentment because *her man* was beside her, inside her, around her, sharing it all with her... and she was not alone.

Eventually they stirred themselves and barbecued a dinner of sorts. The fine steak was somewhat charred, tomatoes collapsed into soggy messes, onions were fried almost out of existence, the bananas were completely underdone and the pineapple was forgotten. It was the best meal they had ever eaten. The bread buns were perfect.

After they cleaned up, they went for a stroll along the beach to look at the stars and enjoy the sight and sound of the sea. They talked of other beaches, other seas, other stars, sharing their feelings about the places they had been in years gone by, sharing their minds and spirits and finding chords of empathy that deepened and broadened their pleasure in walking side by side.

But the need for a more physical expression of intimate bonding grew stronger and stronger, and in mutual accord they returned to the flower bed in Nick's caravan. They made love and talked and laughed and slept intermittently for a few hours. In the grey pre-dawn light, Keira suggested that it would be nice to watch the sunrise from the headland at the end of the beach. Nick agreed it was a fine idea.

It was quite a stiff climb up the steep rock surface, but their feet were light and sure this morning, and there was a sublime confidence in their togetherness. They made it to the top in good time. Shafts of gold from the rising sun were just beginning to send glittering streaks across the sea and into the sky. Nick slid his arms around her waist and pulled her against him as they watched the dawning of a new day... a new beginning.

Keira sighed in deep contentment and dropped her head against Nick's shoulder. "Tired?" he asked, rubbing his cheek over the silky softness of her gleaming hair.

It was funny, Keira thought, but being in love seemed to stop you from being tired. "A bit," she said, so he would keep cuddling her.

His arms pressed her into snuggling closer to him. "I've never felt more alive in my life," he mused softly, his breath wafting through her hair with a sigh of deep pleasure.

"Me, too," Keira whispered.

"You feel it also?"

The strangest feeling of shyness came over her. "Yes," she breathed, wondering why someone like her who had been everywhere, done everything—well, almost everything—should suddenly feel shy with someone with whom she had shared the deepest intimacy.

Movement caught her eye and she instantly pointed to it in excitement. "Look, Nick! Dolphins!"

"A whole school of them," he cried in delight.

"Aren't they beautiful?" Keira breathed.

"Yes, very beautiful."

The deep throb in his voice somehow made the comment personal. Everything this morning seemed personal, as though it was all made just for them to share and enjoy. There was a long harmonious silence as they watched the wondrous animals of the sea cavort over the waves, as if they, too, were greeting the new day with a joyous sense of life.

"Justin is not always wrong," Nick suddenly declared.

Keira frowned at this jarring note. Keira wasn't sure about that. Maybe Justin *was* always wrong. But family was family. She owed her cousin support. "No, he's not always wrong," she said stoutly.

"In fact," Nick amended, "at times he can be astonishingly right."

Keira couldn't see where this was leading. Although she was loath to move from her nestled position, she twisted her body a bit so that she could look at Nick's face. He smiled at her but the smile was a little crooked and strained. The blue eyes seemed intensely watchful as they held hers.

"Don't you agree?" he asked.

"Mmm." A non-committal course seemed wisest.

"Then I suppose we should do what he said," Nick pressed lightly.

Keira's mind was not overly keen on accepting numbers and military operations, which was a fair summary of anything Justin put forward. To get a better grasp of what Nick had in mind, she asked, "What do you think Justin said?"

"He said something about us getting married. If I remember correctly, shotguns were to be used."

"No, Nick." No-one was going to pressure her into marriage, with or without a shotgun. The decision for or against such a relationship was definitely a matter of free choice.

"Try saying yes," Nick suggested, smiling his way into her heart again.

Was he being serious? "No, Nick," she said, wondering why he should feel so urgent about it.

"Why not?"

"We hardly know each other," she pointed out.

"We know enough. All that really matters," he argued.

There was definitely a serious gleam in his eyes. "I'll think about it," Keira said cautiously.

"I love you."

Her heart pounded its response. "That helps," she conceded.

"You're *the one* for me," he said with strong conviction.

"That's a lovely thought, Nick," she encouraged.

"Think of spending our lives together, getting to know more and more about each other, a surprise every day, and gradually learning to adjust so we fit together better and better."

"It could be exciting," she mused.

"More exciting than anything we've done before," he persuaded.

"Yes." She nodded, perfectly happy to be persuaded.

"People call me a gambler, but I'm not. When I decide to do something, the dividends can be enormous."

"I'm starting to believe you."

He moved her within his embrace so that she was facing him properly. "Try kissing me this way," he suggested.

"Okay." Keira was perfectly amenable to this kind of trial.

Nick kissed her, long and slow and erotically teasing. "What did you think of that?" he asked.

"Try it again, Nick. Just to be sure," she said dreamily.

He did, adding a few sensational refinements that were positively dizzying. "Marriage is the only answer," he said deviously.

"Perhaps you're right," Keira said, offering her lips to his again. "You need a woman."

"A special woman." He pressed the words onto her tongue. It was wicked what he could do with his tongue.

"I might be able to do the job," she gasped.

"You're the only one who *can* do the job," he insisted, teasing her some more.

Her nerve endings were shrieking out to be fed as only he could feed them. "I must be going slightly crazy—"

"I've never seen anyone more sane."

"—but I think I might marry you."

"Which goes to prove how eminently sensible you are," he said passionately, and his next kiss sent all her nerve endings into a wild dervish of wanton excitement.

They made love on top of the headland with all the world stretched out below them.

Am I dreaming this? Keira thought. Her mind told her she must be dreaming because everything was too exciting and beautiful and perfect to be true. She hugged Nick closer as wave after wave of pleasure suffused her body.

"Keep me dreaming," she whispered into Nick's ear. "Keep me dreaming all my life."

CHAPTER ELEVEN

A DAIMLER MOVED OFF the Pacific Highway, taking the turning to Forster through which it had to travel before making its way to Boomerang. The guiding hand on the steering wheel belonged to Justin Rigby Brooks. Beside him sat his wife, Louise. Spread comfortably on the back seat was Colonel Winton.

Keira was heavily on the minds of Justin and Louise. A rapprochement was in order, now that everything had been sorted out. And who was to know where Keira might disappear to next if they didn't catch her in Boomerang? Justin had decided that they couldn't count on his cousin being predictable for more than a day or two. Best to strike while she was still within striking distance.

The colonel's mind automatically shied away from the thought of approaching that dangerous young lady. Impossible to avoid this one last meeting with her, but an hour or two should not constitute too much of a danger if he was careful and kept well away from her. He knew enough, now, to avoid the worst situations.

He immersed himself in viewing the incredibly foreign countryside. Totally different from England, he kept thinking, but the natives were very friendly when they weren't being violently aggressive. Louise Brooks was really charming, and the offer of this trip up to the Gold Coast of Queensland was certainly a handsome apology for the injury she had done him. Of course, the colonel was aware that her working for Nick Sarazin had contributed to her concern over his welfare, but that was only right and proper and he had no complaints at all about this interesting compensation.

Neither Keira nor Nick had any premonition that a visitation was about to descend on them. In their own good time they came down from the headland, their appetites well sharpened for breakfast. They demolished a heap of bacon and eggs, changed into swimming costumes, then lay on the beach to soak up some sun.

"You didn't tell me where you've been since I dropped you at the Regent," Nick remarked in mild curiosity. Now that Keira was here, it was of no consequence, but he was interested in everything about her. "I thought you'd come straight to Boomerang," he added, smiling to show her he meant no criticism of her movements.

"I meant to, but I got a bit sidetracked," she explained. "I thought I'd come through the wine district of Pokolbin, and I met some people there who worked for Balloons Ahoy. They were short a helper, and oddly enough, one of the things I've never done is go riding in a balloon. Have you been up in one, Nick?"

"Mmm, one New Year's Eve party, greeting the new year."

They talked about the pleasures of sailing silently along in the early morning sky, and found total agreement once again. Nick thought about the fatal tragedies there had been from ballooning in recent times and thanked his lucky stars Keira had arrived safely at Boomerang.

He knew he could never stop her from doing anything she wanted to do, but he decided then and there that if it was anything dangerous, he would be glued to her side, and if they got killed, they got killed together. He did not expect life would ever be dull with Keira.

Which, of course, made her even more *the one* for him. What he had to do was get her married to him very fast, so he could always be by her side to take care of her. Now that he'd found the flower of his life, he was not about to lose her or let her be injured in any way. Not if he had anything to do with it.

Every so often, Keira obeyed a compelling urge to run a hand over a part of Nick's anatomy. This was to reassure herself that the dream was still going on and acquiring a definite feel of reality. Nick smiled a lot. There was no part of him that Keira didn't find attractive. Eventually he suggested they have a swim. The water was closer than their caravans. It helped to lower their burning temperatures.

Having decided they had had enough sun and sea for a while, and that a long cool drink was in order, they walked hand in hand up the sand-dune to the park.

Keira's yellow costume was a classic one-piece racer, cut high on the hip, with a scooped neckline and secure straps over the shoulder. The thin nylon stretch material enabled it to be packed into the size of a pocket handkerchief. It was a perfectly practical swimming costume, and relatively modest ... when it was dry. Wet, it tended to emphasise Keira's rather lush femininity, faithfully outlining form, shape and curvature.

Colonel Winton, seeing her come over the dune from the beach, wandered slightly off the path towards the caravan that had been pointed out as Keira's. He tripped over a tent-peg, crashed into a camp stool, rolled off onto a metal bar and received a significant and painful injury.

His companions gave him no assistance. Justin and Louise had both stopped dead in their tracks, amazed at the sight of the man who held Keira by the hand. Nick Sarazin was the last man on earth they had expected to see with Keira.

"Oh, hell!" Nick said slowly. He had seen Justin and Louise first. His hand tightened around Keira's. "Here's trouble!"

Keira glanced up and instantly identified what Nick was talking about. Her lateral vision picked up the body of Colonel Winton rolling on the ground. "Louise has been at it again," she murmured, wondering if it was Louise's warlike nature that appealed so deeply to Justin and his military mind.

"Will we make a run for it?" Nick suggested. "See if we can escape?"

It was an attractive idea, but family was family. "I think we have to face the music, Nick," Keira decided.

"Yes," he agreed with a sigh of resignation. "I guess we have to."

His heart didn't appear to be in it. Neither was Keira's. Justin she could handle, but Louise was a fairly scary prospect. Colonel Winton was struggling to his knees, his forehead bent to the ground as though in the deepest prayer to be delivered from all further suffering. At least he couldn't say it was her fault this time, Keira reflected with some relief. She hadn't been anywhere near him.

"What are we going to say?" Nick asked her.

"That it's all your fault?" Keira suggested hopefully.

"That might not be the wisest course," Nick said grimly. He, too, had picked up the contorted figure of Colonel Winton grovelling on the ground.

They made their approach in gloomy silence. A face-to-face confrontation could not be avoided, but at ten paces from her cousin and his wife, Keira's feet limped to a halt. So did Nick's. Both of them had good defensive instincts. Room to manoeuvre was essential if battle was to be joined.

Louise's expression was not projecting peace in our time. It was reserved, stern-faced, unsmiling. Justin was looking confused, suspicious and disapproving. However, he was the first to take the initiative, thereby demonstrating that military minds dictated that moves should be made to resolve sticky situations.

"This is a little embarrassing," he managed to grind out.

"Yes," Nick agreed, just as solemnly.

"Don't be a fool, Justin," Louise said airily, her head tossing high. "Why should it be embarrassing for me to meet Keira for the *first* time?"

A smile lit her face. She advanced on Keira, her arms outstretched in every appearance of a welcoming gesture, her dark eyes flashing what looked like delight in this meeting.

Keira darted a nervous glance sideways, looking for an escape route. Louise could be deceptive. Keira had seen how fast she was capable of moving. There could be a lot of pain for her in this encounter.

Louise gave her no chance. She threw her arms around Keira, embracing her warmly. "Oh, it's so wonderful to see you at last! After all this time!" she gushed with bubbly enthusiasm.

Keira was not slow to catch on. She hugged her cousin-in-law in warm response. After all, Delilah had not been Keira, and there was absolutely no need to remind Louise that this was the *second* time they'd met.

"I'm so sorry about not having made it to your wedding," Keira offered with sincere apology.

"I understand," Louise said firmly.

"It was a sheikh," Keira explained limply.

"Unavoidable in the circumstances," Louise agreed.

"Thank you for being so understanding," Keira said with deep gratitude.

"That's what family is for, isn't it?" Louise asked. She stepped back and gave Keira a firm smile.

"Oh yes. Definitely. Very definitely," Keira agreed.

"I'm pregnant," Louise confided to them and the world in general.

"Is that, uh, good news?" Keira asked diffidently.

"Oh yes," said Louise. "That is definitely good news. Isn't it, Justin?"

"Yes, dear." Justin stepped forward very smartly and put his arm around his wife's shoulders. "The very best news," he added with intense fervour.

"This year," said Louise, "I'm devoting myself entirely to good news. Aren't I, Justin?"

"Yes, dear. Only good news. This is the year you only hear good news."

"Ah," said Nick. "I've got some good news."

The colonel staggered around from behind a caravan. "Dangerous," he said. "Totally, recklessly, foolhardily dangerous. Should be banned."

The good news people ignored these unharmonious comments.

"Keira and I are going to be married," said Nick.

Louise's eyes flashed brightly.

"This had better not be some kind of joke," Justin said belligerently.

"It's no joke," Nick said hastily, and turned to Keira for support. "Is it, Keira?" He put his arm around her shoulders to emphasise *their* togetherness.

"It's not a joke," Keira agreed.

"Then," said Louise with determination, "that's good news!"

"Recklessly dangerous," said the colonel, but the good news people did not hear him.

Peace and harmony had been established.

Justin was shaking Nick's hand and welcoming him into the family.

Keira, having privately given Louise top marks for diplomacy, had reached the conclusion that Justin had certainly met his match in his wife. He was saying how lovely Louise looked, and how she was obviously going to be one of those lucky women whose beauty was enhanced by pregnancy. Which, of course, was good news.

IT WAS THREE MONTHS before the wedding took place. Keira had been in no rush. In her own mind she was certain what her feelings were for Nick, but she wanted to be certain that Nick was certain, too. If he wanted to change his mind, he could. No pressure, no obligation, free choice.

Nick didn't want to change his mind. He appeared quite impatient with what he considered was a very long delay. However, as Keira pointed out, she had been away from home for five years, and she wanted to give Auntie Joan and Uncle Bruce some family time before taking off with a husband.

Besides, there was the important business of meeting Nick's family and being accepted by them. "They might not think I'm respectable enough for you," she said doubtfully.

"Since I'm not respectable either, they'll think we're perfectly suited," Nick declared with confidence.

He was right. They all seemed to think she was the one for Nick. Their thinking, Keira decided, was probably influenced by Nick's obsessive devotion to her. He never shifted from her side, which was fine by Keira. That was precisely where she liked having him.

They invited Colonel Winton to stay for the wedding, but having done what he had come to Australia to do—the TV advertisements were all on film—he declared he had to go home to England. In fact, he intended to retire to a small and ancient fishing village on the Cornish coast. There he could close the door on the world and never come out again. It was far too dangerous.

Keira had a quiet word with Nick, and true to his generous nature, Nick ensured that the colonel had a first-class seat on his flight to London. The colonel's parting words were that he hoped that nothing unseemly would happen at the wedding, and he wished Nick all the luck in the world—all the *good* luck—because he was definitely going to need it.

Apart from a few photographers falling over each other, nothing untoward occurred at the wedding. The church was filled with flowers. It was a happy occasion. A memorable occasion.

The family on Keira's side wondered how matters would finally end up, Keira being Keira, but she certainly made a stunningly beautiful bride this once, and they were very proud to own her as one of them. Although, as Justin said, no-one else—to their knowledge—had ever made Keira cry, so Nick Sarazin might do the impossible and make her happy enough to settle down. But one simply never knew with Keira. Totally unpredictable.

Everyone on Nick's side of the family nodded knowingly as he spoke the words, ''Till death do us part.'' Nick always did what he wanted to do and he certainly had no intention of ever letting his bride go anywhere without him at her side. That was totally predictable.

Nick smiled as he slid the gold wedding ring on Keira's finger. Her sea-green Lorelei eyes swam up at him. His blue eyes promised her that the world was their oyster, and they would ride the king tide together for the rest of their lives.

Keira smiled back.

She knew how it would end up.

She had her man.

Nick Sarazin was the one.

Harlequin Presents®

is

- ✓ exotic

- ✓ dramatic

- ✓ sensual

- ✓ exciting

- ✓ contemporary

- ✓ a fast, involving read

- ✓ terrific!!

Harlequin Presents—
passionate romances
around the world!

WELCOME TO

The quintessential small town where everyone knows everybody else!

Finally, books that capture the pleasure of tuning in to your favorite TV show!

GREAT READING...GREAT SAVINGS...AND A FABULOUS FREE GIFT!

Each book set in Tyler is a self-contained love story; together, the twelve novels stitch the fabric of the community. The covers honor the old American tradition of quilting; each cover depicts a patch of the large Tyler quilt.

With Tyler you can receive a fabulous gift ABSOLUTELY FREE by collecting proofs-of-purchase found in each Tyler book. And use our special Tyler coupons to save on your next TYLER book purchase.

Join your friends at Tyler for the sixth book, SUNSHINE by Pat Warren, available in August.

When Janice Eber becomes a widow, does her husband's friend David provide more than just friendship?

If you missed *Whirlwind* (March), *Bright Hopes* (April), *Wisconsin Wedding* (May), *Monkey Wrench* (June) or *Blazing Star* (July) and would like to order them, send your name, address, zip or postal code, along with a check or money order for $3.99 (please do not send cash), plus 75¢ postage and handling ($1.00 in Canada) for each book ordered, payable to Harlequin Reader Service to:

In the U.S.
3010 Walden Avenue
P.O. Box 1325
Buffalo, NY 14269-1325

In Canada
P.O. Box 609
Fort Erie, Ontario
L2A 5X3

Please specify book title(s) with your order.
Canadian residents add applicable federal and provincial taxes.

TYLER-6

BIG SUMMER READ

Summer Reading At Its Best

In July, Harlequin and Silhouette bring readers the Big Summer Read Program. Heat up your summer with these four exciting new novels by top Harlequin and Silhouette authors.

SOMEWHERE IN TIME by Barbara Bretton
YESTERDAY COMES TOMORROW by Rebecca Flanders
A DAY IN APRIL by Mary Lynn Baxter
LOVE CHILD by Patricia Coughlin

From time travel to fame and fortune, this program offers something for everyone.

Available at your favorite retail outlet.

BSR

"GET AWAY FROM IT ALL" SWEEPSTAKES

HERE'S HOW THE SWEEPSTAKES WORKS

NO PURCHASE NECESSARY

To enter each drawing, complete the appropriate Official Entry Form or a 3" by 5" index card by hand-printing your name, address and phone number and the trip destination that the entry is being submitted for (i.e., Caneel Bay, Canyon Ranch or London and the English Countryside) and mailing it to: Get Away From It All Sweepstakes, P.O. Box 1397, Buffalo, New York 14269-1397.

No responsibility is assumed for lost, late or misdirected mail. Entries must be sent separately with first class postage affixed, and be received by: 4/15/92 for the Caneel Bay Vacation Drawing, 5/15/92 for the Canyon Ranch Vacation Drawing and 6/15/92 for the London and the English Countryside Vacation Drawing. Sweepstakes is open to residents of the U.S. (except Puerto Rico) and Canada, 21 years of age or older as of 5/31/92.

For complete rules send a self-addressed, stamped (WA residents need not affix return postage) envelope to: Get Away From It All Sweepstakes, P.O. Box 4892, Blair, NE 68009.

© 1992 HARLEQUIN ENTERPRISES LTD.   SWP-RLS

"GET AWAY FROM IT ALL" SWEEPSTAKES

HERE'S HOW THE SWEEPSTAKES WORKS

NO PURCHASE NECESSARY

To enter each drawing, complete the appropriate Official Entry Form or a 3" by 5" index card by hand-printing your name, address and phone number and the trip destination that the entry is being submitted for (i.e., Caneel Bay, Canyon Ranch or London and the English Countryside) and mailing it to: Get Away From It All Sweepstakes, P.O. Box 1397, Buffalo, New York 14269-1397.

No responsibility is assumed for lost, late or misdirected mail. Entries must be sent separately with first class postage affixed, and be received by: 4/15/92 for the Caneel Bay Vacation Drawing, 5/15/92 for the Canyon Ranch Vacation Drawing and 6/15/92 for the London and the English Countryside Vacation Drawing. Sweepstakes is open to residents of the U.S. (except Puerto Rico) and Canada, 21 years of age or older as of 5/31/92.

For complete rules send a self-addressed, stamped (WA residents need not affix return postage) envelope to: Get Away From It All Sweepstakes, P.O. Box 4892, Blair, NE 68009.

© 1992 HARLEQUIN ENTERPRISES LTD.   SWP-RLS

"GET AWAY FROM IT ALL"

Brand-new Subscribers-Only Sweepstakes

OFFICIAL ENTRY FORM

This entry must be received by: June 15, 1992
This month's winner will be notified by: June 30, 1992
Trip must be taken between: July 31, 1992—July 31, 1993

YES, I want to win the vacation for two to England. I understand the prize includes round-trip airfare and the two additional prizes revealed in the BONUS PRIZES insert.

Name _____

Address _____

City _____

State/Prov._____ Zip/Postal Code_____

Daytime phone number _____
(Area Code)

Return entries with invoice in envelope provided. Each book in this shipment has two entry coupons — and the more coupons you enter, the better your chances of winning!

© 1992 HARLEQUIN ENTERPRISES LTD.   3M-CPN

"GET AWAY FROM IT ALL"

Brand-new Subscribers-Only Sweepstakes

OFFICIAL ENTRY FORM

This entry must be received by: June 15, 1992
This month's winner will be notified by: June 30, 1992
Trip must be taken between: July 31, 1992—July 31, 1993

YES, I want to win the vacation for two to England. I understand the prize includes round-trip airfare and the two additional prizes revealed in the BONUS PRIZES insert.

Name _____

Address _____

City _____

State/Prov._____ Zip/Postal Code_____

Daytime phone number _____
(Area Code)

Return entries with invoice in envelope provided. Each book in this shipment has two entry coupons — and the more coupons you enter, the better your chances of winning!

© 1992 HARLEQUIN ENTERPRISES LTD.   3M-CPN